Tempting Sinner

King of Hades MC Series, Volume 2

Lexy Timms

Published by Dark Shadow Publishing, 2022.

This is a work of fiction. Similarities to real people, places, or events are entirely coincidental.

TEMPTING SINNER

First edition. April 27, 2022.

Written by Lexy Timms.

BOOK TWO
TEMPTING SINNER

USA TODAY BESTSELLING AUTHOR

LEXY TIMMS

By Lexy Timms

Copyright 2022 By LEXY TIMMS

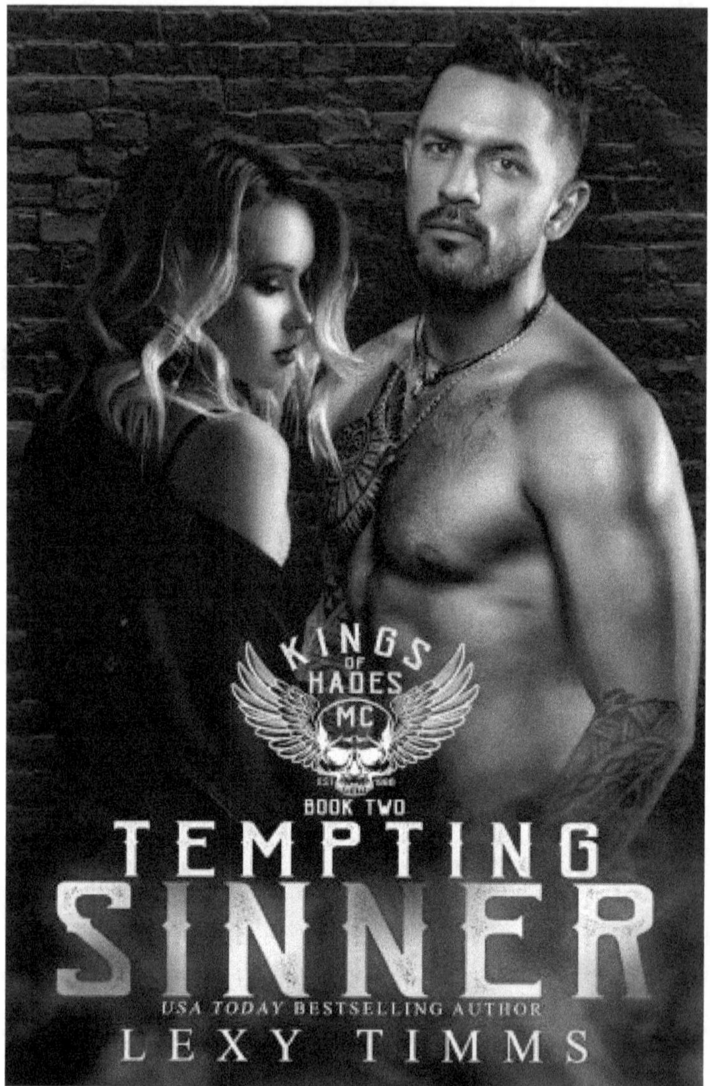
KINGS OF HADES MC
BOOK TWO
TEMPTING
SINNER
USA TODAY BESTSELLING AUTHOR
LEXY TIMMS

This is a work of fiction. Names, characters, places, brands, media, and incidents are either the product of the author's imagination or are used fictitiously. Any resemblance to an actual person, living or dead, events, or locales is entirely coincidental. The author acknowledges the trademarked status and trademark owners of various products referenced in this work of fiction, which have been used without permission. The publication/use of these trademarks is not authorized, associated with, or sponsored by the trademark owners.

Tempting Sinner

King of Hades MC Series #2

Copyright 2022 by Lexy Timms

Cover by: Book Cover by Design[1]

Find Lexy Timms:

LEXY TIMMS NEWSLETTER:
https://www.lexytimms.com/newsletter
Lexy Timms Facebook Page:
https://www.facebook.com/LexyTimms
Lexy Timms Website:
http://www.lexytimms.com

Want to read more...
For **FREE**?
Sign up for Lexy Timms' newsletter
And she'll send you updates on new releases, ARC copies of books
and a whole lotta fun!
Sign up for news and updates!
https://www.lexytimms.com/newsletter

King of Hades MC Series

Book 1 – Sinner

Book 2 – Tempting Sinner

Book 3 – Enticing Sinner

Tempting Sinner Blurb

YOU DON'T HAVE TO DIE to go to hell...

I thought I'd left that life behind.

Instead I just exchanged it for the same one, just a little more dangerous, a little more deadly.

After the gang fight at the bar, and the Kings of Hades MC club clearly the winner, I went home with Jasper in triumph. But when Jasper's brother died, everything falls apart. The one time leader of the Kings was murdered and while we couldn't be sure, it was obvious that the rival gang, the Angel's Death, had something to do with it.

I wanted to help Jasper figure out who was to blame. I was falling for him hard and avenging his brother was the only way he could put the past to rest. Is my ex-lover, Simon "The Reaper" Mortimer, who was to blame? As we dig to get to the truth, I learn something about Jasper's family that could shake him to the core.

Should I tell him and risk the fallout, or keep my mouth shut and leave the skeletons in the closet?

Chapter 1

Jasper

THE LIGHT WASHED OVER me, bright and scathing. There were no shadows in the room, nothing but hospital-like precision and sterile surfaces. But it wasn't a hospital; it was a morgue. I stood, looking down at the body of my brother. He had been beaten and shot, and he lay on the examining table, unattended.

I was having trouble thinking straight. Half an hour had passed since I had been informed of his death, but I didn't know how long he had been gone. I had been with Clara all day. I was supposed to meet my brother and the gang for a strategy session, but I had bailed. I'd had no idea I would never see him again.

Clay was older than me by a few years. He wore his hair longer and his beard was fuller. He worked alongside me at the motorcycle repair shop, and he had a side hustle that involved buying and restoring old bikes. He was the leader of the Kings of Hades Motorcycle Club; he had taken over after the death of our former leader.

That made two leaders dead, within a year. Someone had to pay. I looked down at Clay's face. He was battered and bruised. The purple marks had yet to appear, but there were split marks on his face that I knew came from fists. That and the bullet hole that ripped out his left eye were clear indications that he had been murdered.

I had bullied my way into the morgue by telling them I was the brother of the deceased. The police wanted to talk to me, but I blew them off. I knew they thought that I had more information, but I was just as much in the dark as they were. I couldn't prove that a member of the Angel's Death gang had killed him, but that didn't matter. It was a cold hard fact residing in my gut.

I took off on my bike after declaring that I knew nothing. I drove away, not with any destination in mind, just trying to put distance between myself and the morgue. I felt guilty. If I had shown up to the meeting, maybe none of this would have gone down. Maybe Clay would still be alive and able to lead our gang into the future. Maybe it was my fault. It was possible that the Angels knew where I was because I was sleeping with a woman that one of their gang members was dating.

Dating was maybe a strong word. Clara didn't actually like Simon, and the last time she had seen him, he threatened her with violence if she didn't show up on his arm. It was during that fight at Nomad's bar that I last saw Clay alive. It was debatable who had won. We all went away with visible scars.

I had rescued Clara from a possible death at the hands of one of the rival gang members and beat the guy into a pulp. Hopefully he was unable to rise and had been arrested by the police, but I couldn't be sure about that either.

The rest of the Kings had been pushing Clay to strike back on Vince's murder. That was what the meeting had been about. But had ridden off into the sunset with Clara, turning my back on my brothers both literal and figurative. I was as good as a traitor, although I was sure none of the other Kings saw me that way.

I just needed time to clear my head. I needed to burn rubber, and race away from all my cares. I thought maybe if I drove far enough, hard enough, and fast enough that I could turn back time. I could face my brother and tell him I was sorry. I could agree to join the meeting and help him take down whoever it was who had killed him. Either that, or I could be laying in the morgue alongside him. I wasn't sure which was worse.

I stopped off along the way at a convenience store, purchased a six pack of cheap beer and drank five of them in the parking lot. One can right after another with barely room to breathe, I pounded them down until the world blurred around the edges. Keeping one for the road, I pushed the last of the cans deep into my pocket and climbed back on my ride.

I felt numb. That was better than being hurt, so I went with it. I poured all my energy into driving, not caring where I was going. The last thing I wanted to do was acknowledge what had happened. I was chasing death, even though I didn't realize it. I just wanted to black out and let the angels take me away. It wasn't fair.

Clay was a thousand times more respectable than I was. He had a decent house out in the country, where he worked on his bikes and played pool. He visited our mom with much more regularity than I did. He had a long-term, loving relationship with a waitress at one of our regular haunts.

It was Clay who stopped us from getting revenge on the Angels for the death of our former leader. I supposed that Clay was also technically a former leader, though I didn't want to admit it. I wasn't ready to think about who would be taking the reins next. It certainly wasn't me. I was in no shape to lead anyone and I didn't know the first thing about plotting or managing people.

Clay had a level head on his shoulders. He had argued against retaliation time and time again, telling the Kings he didn't want to see us in jail. There were those who were chomping at the bit, mourning Vince, our fallen comrade. Now that Clay was dead, I was sure that those voices would come back stronger than ever. I didn't think any of the Kings were involved in Clay's downfall. It was an Angel, for sure. But I didn't know which one.

Did it really matter? Weren't they all responsible? Wasn't the next best thing to ride into their club house and start shooting up the place?

I didn't even have the presence of mind to coordinate that attack, although I hoped someone else would.

I just needed to put some distance between myself and my life. In grinding the accelerator to the breaking point, I took a turn too quickly. I thought I could make it, but my judgement was off. Maybe I wanted to fall.

I crashed into a gravel pit, falling from my bike and scraping up my hip. I wasn't wearing any protective gear, although my leather jacket served some use. My jeans tore and the stones dug into my flesh. I felt pain and it was good. I needed that. It was like a physical manifestation of the pain I felt inside and somehow welcome as a result.

I heard my bike sliding across the rocks, the wheels spinning madly. I put my head down as soon as I realized that I had survived. The road lay just feet from my body, a dangerous situation even now that the crash was over.

I had landed on the remaining beer can and for a moment, when I felt the dampness of liquid against my hip, I thought I was bleeding out. Sounds came back to me in batches. First, I heard the motor continuing to run. Then I heard the continual scatter of gravel along the shoulder of the road. And finally, I heard the hiss of the beer leaking from its aluminum container. I wasn't dying, but I didn't feel very good.

Sitting up, I pressed a hand to my head. It was a good sign that I hadn't blacked out, although that was what I really wanted. I thought maybe if I laid down and just went to sleep, some unlucky motorist would run me over without realizing it. I could join my brother and leave it up to the surviving gang members to seek revenge.

But something inside me wouldn't let me take the easy way out. I didn't feel any bumps or bruises on my head. It was a good thing too, since I was drunk and upset. A head injury would earn me a trifecta that I wasn't in any shape to manage.

I climbed gingerly to my feet, testing my weight on the injured leg. Pain flared up as I tried to step on my left foot, causing me to grunt and grind my teeth. I stayed upright, thankfully. Even though I was chasing an early grave, I didn't really want to be stranded.

I limped over to my bike, righting it and brushing gravel from the seat. At that moment, a cop car pulled up. While it was possibly just a patrol car that had nothing to do with Clay's demise, I was suspicious nonetheless. Had they had me under surveillance since leaving the morgue? If so, why did they let me drink and drive?

I touched my pocket, soaking my hand with the remnants of the beer. It was going to be a long night.

"Fuck you," I growled to the police before they even got out of their car.

Both officers came, parking right in front of me and getting out of their respective sides. They had their hands on their revolvers, ready to stop me if I tried anything funny. I was feeling all sorts of ways and not in any kind of mood to be helpful.

"How much have you been drinking?" one officer asked me.

I sniffed. My hip was pounding and my head was foggy. I wanted nothing more than to continue my reckless sprint toward oblivion. I spat in their general direction but it fell short. It took the pair of them all of two seconds to decide that they were going to arrest me.

"Put your hands on your head," one instructed me.

I considered throwing my leg over the side of the bike and tearing off. But even I wasn't that crazy. The thought of a police chase seemed like too much work. I would be better off sleeping in a cell. At least then I would know that I had hit rock bottom.

I dropped the bike and did as I was told. They came around me cautiously, one guy standing in front of me, hand to his hip, the other putting me in handcuffs. To their credit, neither of them pulled their guns. I guessed I just looked like a mess and not like a genuine threat, although they did seem pretty jumpy.

They put me in the back of the patrol car and left my bike by the side of the road. "My bike." It was the first thing I had said in their presence. I watched it disappear into the distance, concerned only about its safety. If someone found it, they could steal it, or destroy it. I realized I hadn't thought things through and I should have tried to make a run for it. At least then I would have had a shot. By giving up, I had placed my baby in danger.

"It'll be impounded," one of the officers said. It wasn't much of a relief, but at least she wouldn't be left out in the open like that for long.

They drove me back into town, to the police station. The city of Stroudville wasn't very big. It didn't have a prison but it did have a jail. The police booked me and shoved me into a cell. It was a drunk tank, designed for those who had imbibed too much to sleep off their headaches.

"Do I get a call?" I mumbled.

The guard didn't reply. There was no use arguing. My head was spinning, not so much from the alcohol but from the fall. I lowered myself onto a bench, stretching out as best I could. There was one other guy in the cell with me, but he was asleep. I put my head down on one side, my knees bent and my feet on the floor.

The room started spinning and I fought the urge to throw up. This was by far the worst night of my life and the night was only getting started. I lay there for more than an hour, not sleeping but unable to move. When I could finally raise my head, I shuffled to the door.

There was a glass window in the metal, streaked with chicken wire. They wanted to be able to see into the cell but didn't want us to get out. I beat against the glass with my hand, making smudge marks. Looking down, I saw that my palm was streaked with blood and sticky with beer. My hip hurt but not as much as it had in the beginning. I was ready to go home.

A guard heeded my call, standing in front of the door. I stood back, letting him open it up. I pressed my eyes shut, trying to silence the ringing in my ears. I was significantly less drunk than I had been when they brought me in and I felt ready to face the music.

"Can I have my phone call?" I asked.

The guard didn't speak but signaled me out into the hall. There were three pay phones I didn't notice before in the hallway right outside. He pointed to one of them, locking the door behind me.

I picked up the receiver. Having gotten myself this far, I wasn't sure who I wanted to call. I couldn't face my mother. If she didn't know that Clay was dead, I didn't want to be the one to tell her. It was cowardly, I knew. But I couldn't deal with that at the moment. I didn't want to call any of the Kings. I wasn't sure if they were engaged in any criminal activity, possibly related to Clay's death. The only other person on my radar was Clara.

I knew her cell phone number by heart. Opting for a collect call, I dialed it and listened as the operator announced my location. There was a good deal of silence on the other end, leaving me to wonder if she would pick up. But after the longest pause in the world, I was relieved to hear her voice.

Chapter 2

Clara

I OPENED MY EYES, EXPECTING to find Jasper still in bed with me. We had spent a wonderful few hours reconnecting and I had fallen asleep. It was good to lie down with another person, especially someone so familiar. Jasper and I knew each other from years back. We used to date, until I decided that I didn't want the excitement of motorcycles in my life, but that had been a mistake.

I thought I wanted a simple guy, someone who could take me to parties and restaurants, someone who could give me the American dream. I imagined how nice it would be to wake up every morning in a two-story home with a white picket fence and a couple of children to take care of. That was until my best friend, Zoe, landed that perfect life for herself.

I went to her wedding and met her husband. I hung out with her throughout her pregnancy and for years while her daughter was grow-ing up. Alice was six and I knew that I wasn't cut out for that life. Zoe was an amazing mom, but I could see the strain in her eyes. She was no longer able to go out clubbing, choosing family game night instead. She all but disappeared from our circle of friends, and I only got to see her because I made the effort to go to her home to hang out.

She was like my sister and I wasn't going to give her up. But that didn't mean I wanted that fantasy for myself anymore. I realized that I liked the freedom of the open road. I liked having fewer responsibili-ties, not to mention that Zoe's experience with pregnancy had me a little bit scared. She lost all control of her own body to a tiny little alien that was adorable but incredibly demanding.

Unfortunately, when I discovered that bikers really were my thing, I ended up going on a few dates with Simon "the Reaper" Mortimer. He hit me up at a biker bar. It wasn't one of those hard-core bars where everyone was involved in gang activities but a much more upscale place that catered to weekend warriors. I was eager to get into some trouble and he seemed like just the thing. We kept it casual until he started inviting me to places that were clearly Kings of Hades' territory. Nomad and Wheelie's diner were off limits to other biker gangs but Simon and his friends didn't seem to care.

At first I thought it was a coincidence, or that they weren't aware of the territory dispute. It quickly became clear that they were showing up at those venues just to irritate Jasper and his crew. And I was just a prop, another method of getting under Jasper's skin.

There was a knock down, drag out fight at Nomad that I escaped only because Jasper came to my rescue. After all that I had to admit to myself that I really wasn't over him. Simon was just a stand in for the man really I loved. And I had displayed that love to Jasper several times over the past few hours, to both of our pleasures.

But when I opened my eyes, Jasper was missing. I was confused at first. Why had he run off? I was expecting to spend the rest of the day with him. Maybe we could make some dinner and watch a movie or hang out in the back yard. I could buy some beers and we could watch the sun set over the neighbor's house.

A little disappointed, I got up and made the bed. When Jasper didn't appear, I took a shower and changed into something new. When he still didn't show up or call, I texted him. I tried to make it sound light at first, a simple, *Hey, where'd you go?*

I waited for a good twenty minutes before following that up with, *Are we getting together later?* It was strange. The whole reason Jasper spent the day with me was because I was worried about being alone. He knew that Simon was focused on me and that it wasn't safe to be by my-self. I just assumed that meant Jasper would want to stick around, but that clearly wasn't the case.

There were crickets from Jasper. I was starting to get worried. I couldn't tell whether I should be pissed or anxious. He might be dead in a ditch somewhere or he might be laughing it up with his buddies. Either way, it didn't spell good things for our relationship.

I tried to relax but the thought of being alone in the house was too worrisome. What had Simon said to me? The Angels knew where I lived. It was a threat and a promise to come back for me if I ever crossed them. Driving away from Nomad on the back of Jasper's bike meant that I was a traitor and I wasn't safe from retaliation.

I called Zoe to ask her if I could spend the night.

"Of course," she said. "But why?"

With a sigh, I told her the whole story about the fight at Nomad, about coming back to my place with Jasper and about the sex. Finally, I told her that he had disappeared and he wasn't answering my texts.

"What do you think it means?" she asked after a moment to process everything I had said.

"I'm worried that he was just interested in sex," I said. It crossed my mind that things might have changed since I last saw Jasper. He was a man, after all; it wouldn't be too big a stretch of the imagination to think that he had charmed his way into my bed.

"What if he was just trying to get back at Simon?" Zoe asked.

"What do you mean?"

"Well, if he knew that Simon liked you—"

"Simon doesn't like me," I corrected her. I was sure of that, at least. Simon had been using me to get to Jasper, that much was obvious.

"But maybe Jasper *thought* Simon did," Zoe concluded, her twisted web a feat of mental acrobatics.

I shook my head. It hurt to think about the situation in that light. I didn't want to consider that Jasper could be so cruel as to use me in the same way Simon was using me. I had given him my body and my love, how could he turn around and abuse me? There had to be some other explanation. I didn't know what it was but I wasn't ready to write him off yet.

Jasper and I shared something meaningful, of that I was sure. It might not be true love, but it wasn't deceitful. He was probably somewhere he couldn't access his phone, maybe in a bar where he couldn't hear it or in a meeting with the rest of the Kings. I couldn't think of a rational explanation, but I knew there had to be one. Jasper wouldn't ghost me like this. There had to be something wrong.

Zoe stayed on the line with me while I packed. I went to my room and pulled out a suitcase. Laying it on the bed, I selected a few outfits. Walking into the bathroom, I packed my toiletries bag. I had told Zoe I was only spending the night but I wanted to be prepared for a few days away. I couldn't tell the future and I didn't want to put myself in the crosshairs by coming back too soon.

Just as I was ready to hang up the phone and tell Zoe that I would be there soon, a phone call from an unknown number broke through. I looked at the screen, trying to figure out where it was coming from.

"I just got a call from some strange number," I told Zoe.

"Answer it," she demanded. "It could be him."

"I'll let you know," I promised, hitting the button to switch the call over.

An operator was on the other end, asking me if I wanted to accept a collect call from the city jail. I groaned. That would definitely answer the question of why Jasper hadn't returned my texts. If he was in jail, they probably took his cell phone away.

I pushed one to accept the charges and listened as Jasper's voice filled my ear. He was angry. I had never heard him angrier. He wouldn't say what the problem was, but I could fill in the blanks all on my own.

He was drunk. Maybe not fall down, pass out drunk, but definitely not sober. I asked him to slow down but he wouldn't. He told me about driving and falling off his bike. He said the bike had been impounded and he had no way home.

"Slow down," I begged him.

"I need you to come bail me out," he demanded.

"Okay," I agreed. "I'm on my way." I hung up the phone and called Zoe back. "He's in jail."

She actually laughed. I didn't feel like I could laugh but it was a good sound to hear. I knew Jasper was hot headed and him being locked up was probably the most reassuring turn of events. That meant he wasn't lying somewhere in need of assistance and he wasn't taking out his aggression on the Angel's Death gang. Maybe that was what landed him in jail in the first place but considering that he was eligible to be bailed out, the charges couldn't be that bad.

It also meant that he wasn't ignoring me. I didn't want to admit that his radio silence had been that painful but the truth was, I had been concerned. Zoe's conjecture that he was using me to get back at Simon had hit home. I had felt washed up and useless. I had felt like nothing we had done together mattered. I had felt used and hurt, but it was all a big mistake.

I grabbed my suitcase, because I didn't know where I was going to land that night, and put it in the trunk of my car. Starting the engine, I took off for the city jail to rescue the man who had come to mean the world to me. No matter what he had done, I was sure we could put it behind us. I never could have imagined the horror that had happened while we slept.

Chapter 3

Jasper

I THOUGHT THAT GETTING in touch with Clara would make me feel better but it didn't. I guessed that Clay's death ate a hole in my heart so big that nothing would ever feel good again. I was consumed by grief and guilt. Even though it was unlikely, I thought that I could have saved him, if only I had taken my head out of my ass long enough to attend that meeting. But my head hadn't been up my own ass, it had been in Clara's bed. That was the problem. She was coming to bail me out but it was partly her fault that Clay was dead.

As soon as the thought crossed my mind, I felt bad for having it. Clara didn't know any better. It was my mistake and mine alone. Still, I wasn't looking forward to seeing her. It was going to be a slap in the face of my brother and everything he stood for. That I would choose sex over him was a bitter pill to swallow.

I was escorted back to the cell and waited for another hour. I didn't know what was taking so long. Clara had said she was on her way. I knew where her house was and it wasn't that far from the jail. It only occurred to me later that she was dealing with the paperwork involved in securing my release.

Another guard came to fetch me, leading me through the hallway and out into the office. Clara was waiting there, holding her keys as if they were a magic talisman that could ward off evil. I knew just how she felt. Hatred was boiling up within me and I needed to let off steam. I was still in shock, still a little bit drunk and definitely angry. At the same time, I could feel my emotions changing.

I walked right past Clara and out into the night. She followed wordlessly, directing me to her car. I got in the passenger seat, fully prepared to drive home in silence. She started the car without a word, seeming to catch on to my despair. But as she pulled out of the parking lot, she turned to face me.

"What happened?" she asked.

"I don't want to talk about it."

"Where were you?"

"I said I don't want to talk about it."

"Where's your bike?"

"It got impounded," I muttered.

"You have to tell me," she insisted. "How can I help you if I don't know what's wrong?"

"I don't need any of your help," I grumbled.

She slammed on the brakes. I looked around, startled out of my funk. We were on the road, in the middle of a two-lane boulevard. Thankfully there was no one around at this time of night, but she was taking a big risk.

"What the hell?" I snapped.

"Tell me what is going on!" she demanded.

"It's none of your business."

"I just bailed you out of jail. You're drunk, your bike has been impounded. You left me without saying goodbye and I didn't know where you went. I thought you might have been hurt or that you were having second thoughts about us..." She trailed off, putting her head down into her hands.

"Drive," I commanded.

She sniffed, resurfacing to put the car back into gear.

I sighed. I didn't want to tell her about Clay. I thought if I said the words out loud it would make them real. If I just continued to ignore it, maybe it would all just go away. Maybe I would wake up the next morning and call Clay and he would be fine. We could get together at

Wheelie's for coffee and pancakes. It was a nice fantasy but I knew it was all a lie. Clay was never coming back and telling Clara what happened wasn't going to make a bit of difference.

"Clay is dead," I heard myself say. I didn't like the words. They sounded raw and hollow, as if they came from somewhere else. There was no explanation, no discussion of the morgue or how he looked lying on the slab. It was just a fact. There was no emotion attached. But at the same time, it was a devastating truth, one that Clara was sure to sympathize with.

She pulled over. We had only driven a quarter mile from the police station when she turned into the parking lot of a dentist's office. I didn't want to look at her. I stared straight ahead, realizing that she needed some time to digest the news. She was quiet for so long, I chanced a look in her direction.

She stared at me with a look of horror and reverence. There were no words of comfort or any attempt to hug me. She was as shocked as I was and grappled to understand this macabre turn of events. I appreciated her silence. Her reaction was just what I needed. For some reason, her inability to process the news meant that I wasn't alone. It was exactly how I felt.

"I don't understand," she said finally.

"He's dead," I repeated. "Murdered. By the Angels."

"How do you know?"

"Because I saw him!" I yelled, punching the ceiling of her car with a vengeance.

She jumped, gripping the steering wheel reflexively. "Oh my... Jasper, I'm so sorry—"

I cut her off. "Don't."

"But he—"

"Don't. Take me home."

She inhaled, squeezing her eyes shut. I could see that she wanted to say more, but there was nothing to say. She pulled out of the parking lot and onto the road, making every turn carefully and obeying the speed limit.

When we reached my house, she pulled up to the curb. I felt the exhaustion of the day take hold and wanted nothing more than to go inside and crawl under the covers. But I knew that sleep would elude me. I didn't feel worthy of sleep. How could I sleep when my brother was in the morgue?

"Do you want me to come in?" Clara asked.

I inhaled sharply. If I was going to be kind to myself and to her, it would be nice to have some company. I didn't want to be alone. I had completely forgotten about her situation and how I promised I wouldn't leave her at the mercy of the Angel's Death gang. All my thoughts were consumed with Clay, how I had betrayed him and left him to die alone. It was haunting and the worst part about it was that I knew I deserved to suffer.

"No," I replied finally. "I wouldn't be very good company."

"I'm not looking for company," she insisted. "I'm not sure you should be alone."

"I'll be fine," I lied.

Looking over at her, I remembered how special she was to me. I hated that she had taken me away from Clay in his time of need but that wasn't her fault. She didn't know what the Angels were up to any more than I did.

I leaned over and kissed her. It was a start, anyway. Her lips were soft, and they reminded me of all the good times we'd had. Letting myself get drawn in, I relaxed for the first time since hearing the news. My future was with Clara, that was for sure. I just wasn't sure that I had a future, or if I even deserved one.

Breaking off the exchange, I climbed out of the car. Slamming the door behind me, I walked to my front door. It was the worst day of my life but there I was, returning home safe and sound. It didn't feel real. I was sure that at any moment, the Angels would jump me or I would wake up in a field somewhere bruised and bloodied. If only that were true. Anything would be better than reality. Putting my back to the one person who truly loved me, I walked through the front door. Sitting down on the couch, I closed my eyes. I would just rest for a moment then I would take up the task of berating myself.

Luckily, it worked and I was able to fall asleep. In my dreams, I forgot all about Clay's death and the gang warfare that had brought it on. In my dreams, I was living happily ever after with Clara, and Clay was married to his girlfriend, Jenny. It was a perfect fantasy and I lost myself to its comforting arms. It didn't occur to me that I had left my better half out in the dark, alone and at the mercy of the killers.

Chapter 4

Clara

I PULLED AWAY FROM Jasper's house as soon as he got out of the car. I couldn't think straight but I didn't want to linger. If he didn't want me to stick around, I wasn't going to. I could only imagine what he was going through, and I didn't want to add anything to his plate.

I couldn't go home. Seeing as how the Angels had killed Clay, I knew I could be next. There was always Zoe. She had agreed to put me up for the night and I was already packed. Feeling numb, I fought to keep up with my thoughts. There were too many to sort out and they ran through my mind with the speed of a thousand bolts of lightning.

Clay was dead. I still had a hard time believing that. I had just seen him the night before at the bar. He had held his own against Davy, the Angel's leader. There was no indication that he was any worse for wear after the fight. When I drove off on the back of Jasper's motorcycle, Clay was alive and kicking. What happened in the intervening hours? How horrible had it been for him?

I didn't even want to imagine. Simon's threats were enough to spook me, the thought that he might follow through with them was too horrible to imagine. What had been Clay's last thought? What had he seen on his way to oblivion? What was Jenny going to do? Did she know? Would she ever recover or would she become a hollow shell of a woman, destined for loneliness and an early grave?

What would I have done if it was Jasper and not Clay? Would I be able to deal with it? Could I deal with Clay's death? I didn't know if I could. It was hitting far too close to home.

I realized I needed more information. I wanted to know the who, what, where, when, and why of the crime. I wanted to understand so I could help Jasper through this rough patch and put him on the road to recovery. Who, other than the police, would know such things?

I needed to track down another member of the Kings. When it happened, Jasper had obviously been with me. He was blaming himself, that much was clear. I thought I remembered that there had been some kind of meeting. Jasper had begged off because I didn't want to be alone. He ended up staying at my house and we went upstairs to the bedroom. That must have been around when Clay met his end.

The realization that we had very likely been climaxing when Clay died was a gut punch. I didn't want to think about it but I was almost positive that was how it went down. Had Jasper come to the same conclusion? Was that why he didn't want me to spend the night? Would this deliver a death blow to our blossoming relationship long before it was ever permitted to take roots?

I pulled into a liquor store parking lot and eased my car between several customers. It was still early, even though so much had happened that night. It wasn't yet midnight and the place was hopping.

I noticed three college guys carrying a twenty-four pack each, on their way to some party. There was a loving couple who were having trouble keeping their hands off each other for the time it took to buy a bottle of wine. And there was a group of teenagers hanging around outside, trying to bribe or beg someone to purchase something for them.

I turned the car off and pulled out my phone. Trying to think of the rest of the gang members, I could only come up with a few. They were all friends of Jasper and Clay, and I had seen them around numerous times. But I wasn't officially part of the group and even though we were all familiar, I didn't have anyone's contact information.

There had to be a way to get someone's phone number, though. Maybe one of the guys was on social media. I opened my own account and typed *Kings of Hades MC* into the search bar. I was rewarded with a mention immediately and followed it to the gang's webpage. From there I chose instant message without knowing exactly who I was talking to. I could only hope that the account was monitored and that someone would get back to me with relative speed.

The message I sent was short and simple. *This is Clara. I need to know what happened to Clay.*

Setting my phone down, I waited. Luckily, I didn't have to wait long. Someone had the app installed on their phone and could see my request as soon as I wrote it. In the chat box, a phone number popped up. I pressed it and the phone dialed.

"Hello?" I asked when someone picked up. All I heard for the first few seconds was heavy breathing.

"Clara?"

"This is Clara," I identified myself. "Who's this?"

"Red."

I knew Red. He was a friendly fellow, as friendly as motorcycle gang members go. He wasn't given to yelling a whole lot and he was a little bit older than the rest of them. He had long red hair and blue eyes and for the most part, he was even tempered. I relaxed a little bit.

"Can you tell me what happened?" I asked.

"Where's Jasper?" Red demanded.

"I just bailed him out of jail and took him home," I said.

"Bailed him out of jail for what?" he sounded suspicious.

"Public intoxication."

Red considered the information and I just had to sit tight. I knew he was processing and that he would either tell me what I wanted to know or hang up on me. It looked bad that I had been riding around with Simon from the Angel's Death gang. I could imagine that some of Jasper's crew had an issue with that. I decided to meet the challenge head on instead of waiting for it to bite me in the ass.

"I know you saw me with Simon," I hurried to explain. "But that wasn't a real relationship. I don't want anything to do with him anymore. It was a mistake to get involved. I mostly wanted back into the lifestyle and Simon was there at the right time in the right place. I think he was using me all along."

"You got that right," Red agreed.

"I know," I continued. "And I feel horrible about it. But I need to know what happened to Clay."

"Why?"

"Because I care about him. Because I care about his brother. Because I care about all of you assholes."

Red chuckled and I could sense that I was getting through to him. Just a few more sentences could push him over the edge, allowing him to open up to me. I had the floor and it was time to plead my case.

"Jasper trusts me. He called me to bail him out tonight. What do you think that says about my loyalties?"

"Jasper's not thinking right," Red grumbled.

"I know. He's in pain and he's not dealing with it. I just want to help."

Red sighed before finally letting me in on the details. "We had a meeting, which your boyfriend chose not to attend."

I let it go. There was no reason to argue about calling Jasper my boyfriend. At least we had moved on from assuming I was with Simon.

"We talked about Vince and how we were going to deal with the Angels after the fight." There was a pause and I wanted to reach through the satellite to urge Red on but held my tongue. I had to let him continue at his own pace. "We all rode out around three. Clay went home and the bastards must have been waiting for him there. Cade went over to try to talk some sense into him. There was an argument about how rough we should be with the Angels. Clay wanted to be cautious and Cade wanted to go all in."

I was learning a whole lot about inner gang politics. The mere fact that there were disagreements within the ranks told me more than I ever knew before. I kept silent, willing Red to continue. He picked up the thread a moment later, finishing the sordid tale.

"Cade found him and called me. I raced over there and, uh, we... removed any incriminating evidence before calling the police."

That made sense, I supposed. I didn't know what exactly the gang was into but I knew they weren't strictly on the right side of the law. Clay might have had texts or emails alluding to an attack or maybe even things that had been stolen inside his house. His friends were looking after his memory and protecting those who were still alive. Plenty of people did it, although I didn't know any of them. This was actually my first experience with violent death, and I didn't like it one bit.

The last time I saw Simon, he had threatened me. And then merely hours after that threat, he or someone close to him murdered Clay in cold blood. It was too close to home, too horrible to comprehend. I sat there with my phone in my hand, trying to think of something to say.

"Did he suffer?" I heard myself ask. It was a stupid question; the man had been murdered. Yet I thought there might be some comfort had if it was a clean shot to the head or something equally quick and relatively painless.

"Yes," Red replied, shattering my last hope.

"I'm so sorry." I knew that he was feeling the loss more than I was. Maybe less than Jasper, because no one else had known Clay for their whole life, but Red had been riding with Clay for at least a decade. I was the one on the outside and the murder ate away at my soul. I could only imagine what it was like for the gang.

"Yeah, well, shit happens," Red spat.

I closed my eyes. Of course he didn't want my pity. What good would that do him? He couldn't afford to take time off to mourn, or to embrace well-wishers as they came around. He had to be tough. Jasper, on the other hand, wasn't there yet. He was falling apart, drowning his sorrows, pushing people away. I had to find my own path and it wasn't exactly the same as either of the guys'.

I was scared. I felt guilty thinking of myself in a time like this but realistically, I could be next. Jasper wasn't in a caring mood and Red had made his feelings about me clear. I remembered my plan to go to Zoe's house but she had a little daughter. I couldn't live with myself knowing that I had brought any kind of pain or trauma into their lives, so I knew that was no longer an option.

I ended the call with Red. There were no words that I could offer him, so I didn't try. I thanked him for telling me about Clay and I promised that I would stay away from the Angels.

"Good," Red replied. "Because I won't protect you anymore."

I held my tongue. The man was angry and lashing out; he didn't mean to be a jerk. I was lucky that he had decided to trust me enough to give me the information I was looking for. I didn't need to get into a screaming match with him over the phone.

Things had gone from bad to worse. At Nomad the previous night, I was sure that being trampled in a bar fight would be my fate. When we escaped, I thought the police were going to come after us. When neither of those two things happened, I allowed myself to relax enough to enjoy being with Jasper, but it seemed like that was the worst thing I could have done.

Could I have stopped the murder? If I was a better girlfriend to Simon, maybe Jasper wouldn't have felt the need to protect me. He would have been free to attend this meeting, whatever that was, and maybe Clay never would have gone home that afternoon. It was useless thinking, but I couldn't help myself.

I called Zoe to explain that I wasn't in need of a bed anymore.

"Why not?" she demanded.

"I'm feeling better," I lied. I didn't want to tell her that things had gone steeply downhill. I didn't want her to worry about me or send her husband, Patrick, to help. The last thing I wanted to do was put my friends in the crosshairs. Zoe didn't know what I was up against. The Angels weren't fooling around.

"Okay," Zoe sounded suspicious, but she let me go. "The offer is always open if you need it."

"Thanks," I replied, hanging up.

With nowhere else to turn, I decided to get a hotel room for the night. Stroudville wasn't that big, but there were a handful of hotels downtown. Mostly conference venues for out-of-town businesspeople, they were cold and impersonal spaces where people could go to hide themselves. I stayed away from the rent-by-the-hour places. They were in a whole different location, in a seedier side of the city.

I drove straight downtown and eased off onto a wide boulevard that had numerous shops and restaurants. The hotels were spaced evenly throughout the commercial district so that visitors could walk to dinner and pick up some shoes and purses along the way. It was almost midnight and everything was closed.

The hotel I picked wasn't packed. There wasn't a conference or a holiday or an event in town. It was just a regular night and there might have been a dozen cars in the parking lot. Grabbing my suitcase from the trunk, I wheeled it into the lobby.

A young man looked up from his phone and grudgingly took my credit card. I wasn't worried about being tracked. The Angel's Death had a lot going for them but I didn't think they had any law enforcement connections. They gave me a room on the fourth floor and a key card that would let me in.

"There's a pool and a fitness center in the basement," the front desk clerk monotoned. "Fitness center opens at five. Pool opens at ten. Checkout is eleven."

"Thanks," I replied, pocketing my key. I didn't want to talk to him any more than he wanted to talk to me. We were just two strangers passing each other in the night. As long as I didn't put up a fuss, I knew he would forget he had ever seen me.

Reaching my room, I let myself in. As soon as I crossed the threshold, I put my back to the door and collapsed into tears. I was safe.

For the first time since Jasper left that afternoon, I felt like the Angels couldn't touch me. Alone in an anonymous hotel room, I was able to shed the fear of death. But with that freedom came a torrent of grief. Clay Ayers should still be alive. I was the one who had betrayed the motorcycle gang. I was the one who should be lying on that slab.

Chapter 5

Jasper

I ROLLED OVER AND LOOKED at my bedside clock. It was eleven, but I wasn't sure if it was eleven in the morning or eleven at night. The curtains were drawn and the room was dark. I thought I could hear birds chirping outside so that must mean it was daytime.

I ran a hand over my face. How many days had it been since Clay was killed? I couldn't tell. They were all a drunken blur. My mouth tasted like ass and I couldn't remember the last time I brushed my teeth.

My hair was a rabbit's nest on top of my head. My beard was still full of gravel. I had scrapes all down one leg from the fall and I hadn't even bothered to wash them out. It felt like months since I had taken a shower but I didn't want to indulge. Showering, shaving, washing up, taking care of myself, it all felt pointless.

The only thing I hungered after was beer. As long as I maintained my buzz, things wouldn't hurt so bad. That's what I told myself, anyway. If it was only eleven then I could sleep for a few more hours. Hell, I could sleep for a few more days if I chose.

My phone beeped and I grabbed at it. Basically ignoring every message that came in, I did take the time to read them. I had sent a message to the garage early on the morning after Clay was killed. My message was short and to the point.

Clay is dead. I'm not coming in today. That was it. Let the boss figure out the rest on his own. Of course, he had responded with condolences and a promise to keep my job for me whenever I was ready to come back. He didn't ask me how Clay died and I wondered if he already knew. Our boss wasn't in a gang – or at least, I didn't think he was in a gang – but he often seemed knowledgeable about things that were going on. It was as if he had his own ties to the underworld and was just living life out in the open as a sort of cover. I was too foggy headed to worry about him for the time being. The most important person in my life was gone and that was all I cared about.

Clara had texted me the morning after. I opened up the thread just to re-read it. There was a missed call and then her thoughtful opening bid, *How are you holding up?*

I didn't bother to answer that because the question was ridiculous. I wasn't holding up at all. *Are you safe?* I had asked. Getting straight to the point, I just wanted to satisfy my own desires. I had deliberately missed the last meeting my brother would ever hold because I was worried about Clara's safety. It only made sense to check in with her. If she wasn't, then I would have to figure something out.

She responded a moment later with, *Yes. I'm worried about you.*

Don't worry, I told her. There really wasn't anything to worry about. I was just drinking myself into an early grave. It was all I could do not to go barging into the Angels' clubhouse on my own. I might have been outnumbered but at least I would go down fighting. The only thing that stopped me was knowing that action wouldn't bring Clay back. Nothing would bring him back. He was gone forever and it was all my fault.

It had been at least three days since Clara's last text. I couldn't be sure, because I hadn't left my house, but I thought that was an accurate estimate of the time that had passed. I thought about calling her. Maybe I could invite her over and we could patch things up. It wasn't fair to blame her for Clay's death, and I knew it. She was a victim just as much as my brother had been.

Looking around the room, I narrowed my eyes. The place was trashed. There were empty and partially empty beer cans scattered all over the floor. The bed hadn't been made because I never left it. The blackout curtains swallowed up the sun and made the whole place stink like some kind of hothouse.

Ignoring the mess, I pushed my way out into the hall. The disaster continued all the way down the stairs to the living room. Luckily, I didn't have much furniture and since I hadn't changed my clothes in a while, there wasn't a lot of debris. I went through my stash of beer pretty quickly and made one daily trip to the corner store within walking distance to stock up on supplies.

I had ordered a pizza one night but it took me two days to eat it because I didn't feel like I deserved nutrition. Returning home with my arms full after a beer run, I had noticed the absence of a bike beneath my awning. It was heartbreaking. Not only had I lost my best friend since childhood but I had lost my ride as well.

It was in the impound lot and I didn't want to go get it. I didn't have the strength to show my face. I didn't even have the energy to work out at home, leaving the basement gym as the one room in the home that was untouched since before Clay died.

Checking the refrigerator, I thought there might be a beer or two left. I was in luck. Apparently I had passed out before finishing them all off, so there were a few cold ones waiting for me. I popped a tab, swilling the brew. It tasted good and the resulting buzz brought me back to a place of peace.

I finished off the first one and reached for another. Dumping the empty in the sink, I just added to the mess. Popping it open, I emptied half of it down my throat before walking back to the living room.

There wasn't even enough energy left in my body to turn on the television. I sat on the couch and stared at the wall. I was nearly finished with the second drink when the doorbell rang. I rolled my eyes. The last thing I wanted was visitors. Thinking maybe it was the Angels come to finish their violent attack, I got up to answer.

Maybe death had come for me at last, or revenge would be served up on a silver platter. The fact that I wasn't ready for any kind of physical altercation didn't escape me. If it was my enemies, they wouldn't have any difficulty rolling me into a shallow grave.

Some part of me knew that the Angels wouldn't ring the doorbell, though. It could be my mom, which would be even worse. I didn't care. If it was her, I would tell her to go home. I needed to deal with my own grief on my own terms and I didn't have the presence of mind to help even my closest relations see their way through this.

Opening the door, I found Red and Cade. Of all the people who could have come to visit, it was probably best that it was my fellow Kings. None of them were related to Clay by blood but I knew they felt his execution as painfully as I did. First it was Vince, then Clay. We were dropping like flies.

I left the door open without saying anything and walked back into the house. I knew they would follow but I didn't care. I was beyond the pale comforts of well-wishers. Deep into my own nightmare, I couldn't see a way out.

"Jasper," Cade said.

I turned back around and saw them lingering on the front step. "What?"

"Come here," he demanded.

I took another swig of my beer, finishing it off. Crunching the can, I tossed it onto the couch. I didn't care if what was left over in the can stained the fabric. The couch was a thrift store find and my home was a disaster area.

"What?" I repeated.

"Just come here," Cade said again.

I walked back to the door, bleary eyed. The two guys stood aside and pointed to the driveway. Clay's bike sat there waiting for me, its unpolished metal and leather seats exactly as they were when Clay was alive. I turned to Red, uncomprehending.

"We heard your bike was impounded," Red explained. "Figured you needed something to ride."

My jaw dropped. Of all the kind gestures, this one was the most benevolent. What was a biker without a bike? It was true that I missed my ride. I could have been out, tooling around the city, losing myself to the open road. Instead, I was holed up in my house like a hermit, not wanting to risk daylight.

I stepped outside, blinking away the sun. Walking over to the driveway, I ran my fingers along the slope of the engine. I could almost hear Clay talking to me just then. *Ride*, he said. *Take good care of my bike.* I could feel tears begin to bubble up in my throat and clamped them down. It was a noble gesture and one that I knew I would appreciate long after the day was done.

"Thank you," I whispered.

Red came up behind me and put a hand on my shoulder. "It's what he would have wanted."

I nodded.

"Can we come in?" Cade asked, all proper for once.

"Can I stop you?" I grumbled.

The two of them looked at each other in alarm. I didn't know if they actually thought I would turn them away. I just meant that my home was their home and that they were free to come and go as they pleased.

"I'm joking," I clarified.

Cade smiled tightly, preceding me into the house. I walked in behind him and entered the living room. Red took up the rear and closed the door behind him. Surveying the landscape, they each did a double take. I wasn't usually a messy guy. True, I had little to decorate my home but what I had was usually free from clutter.

There were beer bottles strewn all over the place with no attempt to hide my state of mind. They didn't attempt to clean up or anything so rude. Instead, they hovered near the door, not wanting to disturb the scene.

"Do you want a beer?" I asked.

"Sure," Cade said.

"I'm good," Red replied.

"Good," I responded, moving to the kitchen. "Cause I think I've only got one left."

Opening the fridge, I saw that was true. There was a single beverage left in the cardboard box. I wanted it for myself but since I had already offered it to Cade, I handed it over. He took it without a word and opened it.

I already had two in me so it wasn't a huge loss. I would make my daily pilgrimage to the corner store in just a few hours anyway. In the meantime, it looked like my fellow Kings had something they wanted to say.

"What's up?" I asked them.

"We need to talk," Red opened.

"About?"

"About Clay."

"What about him?"

"What are we going to do?" Red asked. "We can't let his death go unchallenged. Aside from the honor of revenge, we'd be setting ourselves up for easy killings if we don't hit back."

"I'm all for killing the bastard," I said, "but which one?"

"Does it matter?" Cade asked.

I shook my head. I was too weary to sort through all the details but something told me it would have mattered to Clay. "I don't think Clay would want us going to jail over a retaliation strike. I think if we're going to do anything, it has to be targeted."

"Fuck targeted," Cade argued. "Let's just ride up to their club house and open fire."

"With what?" I countered. "We don't have heavy artillery."

"We can get it."

"And go down for buying illegal weapons?" Red took up my cause. "For that kind of full-frontal assault, we would need machine guns."

"I could get them," Cade replied.

I looked at him, wondering if he was telling the truth. For all our brushes with the law, we weren't any kind of organized crime family. We didn't use or sell drugs and we didn't have mafia connections. Where Cade thought he was going to come by a large amount of off the books weaponry, I couldn't imagine.

"Clay didn't want us to be killers," I said finally. "We wouldn't be honoring his memory if we let the situation escalate."

"Is that how you feel?" Red asked suspiciously.

"I guess," I muttered. "I haven't really thought about it."

"We need some way to figure out who pulled the trigger." Red stroked his beard thoughtfully. "And I think I've got a way in."

Chapter 6

Clara

I STOOD NEAR THE FRONT door of my house, listening to the installation technician explain how my new security system was going to work. It had been almost a week since I stepped foot in my own home, living out of a suitcase at the fancy hotel. It was eating into my budget and I felt a little bit lost.

I had no anchor and no place to hang my hat. Feeling safe was important, but so was feeling like I owned my own space. I couldn't stay with friends and I couldn't stay with Jasper. The hotel was just a stopgap method and I had to figure out a way to move back home.

During my lunch break at work on Wednesday, I was explaining my situation to a friend. I didn't tell her everything. In fact, I sort of lied. I said that there had been some break-ins in my neighborhood and that I didn't feel safe at home alone. I told her that I had moved my things to a hotel on a temporary basis but I couldn't continue to stay there.

"How long have you been there?" she asked.

"Since the weekend."

"Oh, gosh." She seemed alarmed and I had to pretend that it was probably nothing, that I was overreacting and that I wasn't in any real danger. "Have you thought about getting a security system?"

"A security system?" I pondered.

"There are some real top of the line models that are fairly inexpensive these days," she continued. "My husband got one for his mother. She lives alone."

"What does it do?" I asked.

"It's connected to a call center that monitors your home 24/7. There are sensors on all the doors and windows so that if anybody tries to break in, they'll send the police. You have a code like a PIN that you use to arm it and disarm it but there's also a panic code so you can call the police without having to use your phone."

I liked the sound of it. My colleague gave me the number and I called the company when my break was over. They were very sympathetic as I told them my story about the break-ins. I was their bread and butter it seemed, a single woman living alone who was prone to overreactions.

They sent someone out the next night. I checked out of the hotel after work and met him on the curb. He was dressed in a uniform so that he was easily recognizable as an employee of the security company. He had a green and white van with a friendly looking family painted on the front, all designed to put the customer at ease.

I walked him through the house, pointing out all the doors and windows. He suggested focusing on the first floor, since it was unlikely that an intruder would climb a ladder and enter through a bedroom window. I told him I wanted all the bells and whistles; I didn't care how much it cost.

He shrugged, apparently figuring that it was more money for him. While he worked, I went to my refrigerator to clean out some of the old stuff. There were leftovers from a week ago that smelled horrible. I threw a bunch of things in the garbage and took the bag out to the bin. Tidying up made me feel better. It was a little bit like nesting, coming to terms with my own home again.

After two hours, the technician had installed safety devices on all of my windows and doors. He popped his head in the kitchen to tell me that he was ready to move on to the next stage of the game; the paperwork.

"All the windows have this sensor attached." He showed me one on a living room window. It looked like a little box attached to the windowsill. "When someone opens the window, the alarm will go off." He demonstrated and a blaring siren split the air. Closing the window rapidly, he marched to the front door and tapped in the code. The alarm quieted instantaneously.

"I gave it the starter code but you'll have to change that as soon as I leave," he said, handing me a pamphlet. "There are instructions for how to pick your own code in here. You can change it as often as you like."

I inhaled sharply, already thinking about what my PIN would be.

"The doors are similarly outfitted," the guy continued. "And there are motion sensors in the corners of the living room and the kitchen." He pointed to the ceiling and I could see tiny plastic globes installed. "There's a night setting that will give you five minutes to get upstairs. After that, the alarm will go off if there is any movement downstairs."

"Great," I replied, feeling safer already.

But he wasn't finished. He took me upstairs to the bedroom, where he had installed a small monitor on the wall by the door. Tapping the screen, he showed me visual images of the living room, front and back porches, driveway, and kitchen. He gave me a tablet that would control the whole setup and another booklet on how to use it.

When the explanation part of the process was complete, he hit me with the bill. I had to sign a contract or pay for all the equipment. Since the price tag was exorbitant, I held my breath and signed away. My life was worth another couple hundred dollars a month, I reasoned.

The technician left and I was finally alone. I stood in my living room, breathing in the familiar air. It felt good to be home. I opened the first pamphlet and figured out how to change the code. Without tripping the alarm, I managed to set it to a number I would remember. That was the last thing on the list. No one could get in without my permission, not even the man who installed it.

I was free and safe. There wasn't a lot of food in the house but there was enough for dinner that night. I could go to the grocery store later. If I left home alone and came back, there was a chance that Simon could attack me. Coming and going would be the riskiest parts of my day but inside my castle, I was queen.

I wandered around both upstairs and down, setting things to rights. I cleaned the bathrooms because I wanted them to smell fresh. I tidied my bedroom and fluffed the pillows. I sat down on my bed, gazing over at the monitor. From there, I could see everything, and there were no bad guys lurking in the bushes. Maybe the Angels Death gang would forget about me. Maybe killing Clay had gotten it out of their system and they would leave me alone to live my life. It was a nice fantasy, but I was sure it wasn't true. The day would come when my security system would pay for itself. It did my heart good knowing that there was a whole office full of people watching the feed. Luckily, there wasn't a camera in the bedroom.

Thinking that thought brought me one hundred and eighty degrees back to Jasper. I hadn't heard a word from him since the day after I bailed him out. He hadn't shut me down exactly but he wasn't encouraging of my attention. I let him be, focusing on myself and my situation. I figured he would let me know if he needed something and I trusted that someone would clue me in if anything else happened.

Still, I was curious. He meant a lot to me and I wanted to know that he was okay. More than that, I wanted to see him. I pulled out my phone and sent him a quick text. *How are you?*

I wouldn't have been surprised if he didn't respond and I prepared myself for the disappointment. To my great relief, he texted back almost immediately. *I'm still here. Can you come over tonight?*

I'm still here was good news. At least that meant he hadn't been arrested again and that he was home instead of lying in a ditch somewhere. He wanted to see me! My heart soared at the implications. Maybe we could get past the trauma of Clay's death and begin seeing each other again. It almost felt like we were a couple when he spent the night after the bar fight. It felt so good to reconnect and I was worried that the damage done by his brother's murder was irreparable.

Sure. I replied, nonchalant.

He liked my response and I felt a warm glow growing in my belly. I laid down on top of the covers. Dropping my phone onto the bedside table, I laced my fingers together over my chest.

I remembered the last time I was in this bed. Jasper and I were doing beautiful things together, kissing and rubbing delicious places. I allowed my thoughts to drift back into the past. He was naked beside me, his chest on display. His long hair brushed the pillow and his beard framed his jaw as he gazed down at me, his eyes sparkling with love. I felt the heat as his lips descended onto mine, the soft brush of a kiss sending fire racing through my veins.

I opened my arms and circled his neck, pulling him in close. He leaned over me, as eager to get started as I was. I could feel his hands on my body through my clothing, the erotic phantom lingering in the air.

I turned my hips as if I was pressing into him, feeling his abdominal wall flush against mine. His cock was hard, pressing through the denim of my pants, immune to all barriers. I lowered my hands to my waist, peeling open my fly. Dipping one hand into my underwear, I focused on the memory.

Jasper rode me hard from above. His hands were planted next to my rib cage, his body elongated and pressing me into the mattress. I could almost feel his powerful strokes, the tip of his manhood burrowing deep. I looked up through slitted eyes to the ceiling above me, then closed them tight. Without the benefit of sight, I could almost feel him inside me, rocking toward his conclusion.

We were partners in the bedroom, each one working to glorify the other. I touched myself, sliding the pad of one finger over my clit. My body bounced to the ready, every cell in perfect anticipation of the ritual. I felt myself slide down into the recesses of my mattress, melting out of my physical form. I turned into a being of pure delight, treating myself to the ultimate in personal pleasure.

Jasper was there with me, in spirit. It was his image that I clung to as I teased myself onward. I parted my lips, imagining that I was kissing him. I felt his beard scratch my cheek, imagining the hard wire of his scraggly hair. It was enticing and only spurred my fingers on.

I quickened the pace, dragging my digit through the slick folds of my erogenous zone. I pushed one up inside me and pulled it out again, a poor imitation of what Jasper would be able to do. Squeezing my eyes shut, I clung to his ghost, bucking and writhing beneath him as he worked his magic. He was my best friend, my champion, and my lover. I longed to see him again.

With a desperate gasp, I tossed myself over the edge. My body trembled, waves of relief crashing onto the shore. My breath was hot in my lungs and withering on my lips, giving me all the sensations of a real-life encounter.

I slid my hand free, resting it on my abdomen for a moment. The Jasper in my bed faded, leaving me alone once again. I restored hope with the knowledge that I would see him again very soon, possibly to reunite and continue our love affair. A girl could dream, couldn't she?

Chapter 7

Jasper

HAVING INVITED CLARA over, I thought it best to clean up. Red and Cade went home or wherever else they planned to go that day. I spent an hour walking around the house with a trash bag collecting beer bottles. There were so many that it made me realize just how lost I had been.

I walked through the living room, the kitchen, and even found one on the staircase. In my bedroom, there were dozens lying on the floor and on the bedside table. I found two in the bathroom sink and one in the shower. I didn't even remember throwing it there and I was sure I hadn't washed off since learning about my brother's fate.

When the debris was cleared, I grabbed a sponge and wiped off some of the surfaces. Just using the cleaner underneath the sink made the place smell nicer. I thought about mopping the floor and finally worked up the energy to do it. If I didn't, there would be sticky spots and that wouldn't make a good impression.

There wasn't much I could do about the couch. I flipped the cushions so that any stains were hidden. I picked up my clothing and started a load of laundry and finally got into the shower to scrub all the grief off my skin. It felt good to be underneath the water pressure. The heat burned some of my indecision away.

I was about to ask Clara for a big favor and I needed to set the stage. It was funny, I didn't feel any more put together than I had before my buddies arrived, but the mere act of cleaning was cathartic.

I realized that my life wasn't over, even though some part of me wanted it to be. I couldn't hide in the bottle forever. I owed it to my brother, to my family, and to the rest of the Kings to stand up.

When I was showered, I trimmed my beard. Gazing at myself in the mirror I saw that even a good cleaning couldn't erase the haunted look in my eyes. The reflection was of a beaten man and I didn't like that. I wanted to look mean and focused but the best I could summon was weary. It would have to do; it was the best I had.

I dressed in clean clothes and went downstairs to work on supper. There wasn't anything in the house to feed a woman and I wasn't any kind of a chef. My options were bleak. I could go to the grocery store or I could order out. I opted for the latter, picking a middle of the road meal from one of the delivery services. It cost a pretty penny but Clara was worth it. I also realized that I was hungry, since I hadn't eaten appreciably in days.

When the food arrived, I placed it on the coffee table. It was the only solid eating surface I had in the house. Clara wouldn't mind, though. She knew that I wasn't domestic. I just hoped that I could pull off a halfway decent approximation of a functioning human being.

Red's plan was simple. Since Clara had already gone on a few dates with Simon, she could help us discover who was to blame. It would necessitate a little deception on her part and a willingness to put herself back in harm's way. I would be there for her as much as possible but there might be times she would find herself alone with the rival gang.

I had argued against the plan to begin with. It was too dangerous and Clara was a civilian. She wasn't a member of the Kings and we couldn't ask her to put her neck on the line for us any more than we could ask my mom or Red's mother.

But my friends wore me down.

"She called me the night that Clay was killed," Red shared.

I perked up. This was news to me. I didn't even know that Clara knew Red's number. "What did she say?"

"That she cares about you. That she cared about Clay and wanted to know what happened to him. If you give her an opportunity, I'm sure she'll make the right choice."

"You didn't see her at the fight at Nomad," I argued. "Dom almost choked her."

"She'll be fine," Cade replied easily. "Simon may be a bastard, but he's a guy. He didn't ask her out just because the two of you used to be an item. She's hot."

I narrowed my eyes at my friend, despising his comments. Clara was hot, I wasn't disputing that fact. But I was sure that the motivation behind Simon's interest was less about getting laid and more about getting under my skin.

"We have to protect her," I ordered.

"We will," they replied quickly.

I sighed heavily, my heart reluctant to let Clara get into any danger. Red was right though; she was the best weapon we had at the moment. I would let her decide, and I would support whatever decision she made.

After getting the whole set up ready for Clara, I even called the auto shop. I talked to my boss and explained the situation. He had a lot of questions about what happened and what he could do to help. I told him there wasn't anything anyone could do but that I was planning to come back into work soon. He was glad to hear it and we hung up amiably.

Clay worked at the same place and, like in all our endeavors, he was higher up on the food chain than I was. He was a shift manager and I was just a lowly technician. I wondered if I would be asked to step up. It wouldn't be a bad move. My mom's husband was always on me to make something more of myself, to go out for the promotion.

I thought wickedly about tossing that advice back in his face. I knew this wasn't how he envisioned me getting that promotion. Still, it would satisfy some evil desire deep down to see the guy's face crumble.

I had never liked him and I didn't like how he treated our mom. My mom. I decided to bring it up the next time I saw him, just out of spite.

There was a knock on the door at exactly seven. Clara was nothing if not on time. I straightened up, feeling like I was going in for the tackle. I had to present a competent face and make it seem that my world wasn't falling apart. I sucked in a breath and did a last-minute flight check. I had dinner, the place was clean, I was clean; check, check, check. Opening the door, I was struck again by how beautiful she was.

It wasn't just that we had been together recently. She would have looked gorgeous even if she was a stranger. It was no wonder that Simon had picked her up in that bar. I don't know why I kept away for so long. I had thought she didn't like me, but that wasn't true. She was finding her way back to me in the most convoluted way possible, but the sentiment was still there.

She was empty handed and I could tell she was a little nervous. It had been days since we saw each other and a lot had happened. I gestured toward the living room and she stepped gingerly inside.

"There's a bike in the driveway," she mentioned. "It doesn't look like yours."

"It's Clay's." The words were hard but I spoke them anyway. Swallowing down a wave of sadness, I turned toward the picnic.

"I'm sorry," she said, coming up behind me. She put a hand on my shoulder and somehow that made things worse. I resisted the urge to shake it away. I was supposed to be trying to enlist her help, not engaging in a big emotional fall out.

Clara didn't want to hurt me. She was just trying to be kind. It was me who couldn't take the friendship, who couldn't bring myself to look at her without seeing Clay. It was a painful reminder of my personal failings. I should have been there for my brother. This attempt to find the culprit and punish him was a pale comfort next to seeing Clay alive again.

"I want to thank you for bailing me out," I began. I thought it was best to start at the beginning.

"Of course," she replied. I realized that she would bail me out again and again, as many times as I needed her to. I didn't know if that was a good thing or not. It meant that she was likely to say yes to the plan if she thought it would help. And knowing that, it left the power in my hands. Should I ask her or not? If I knew the answer would be yes, should I even make the request?

"I thought we could have some dinner," I moved aside to let her see the spread.

It wasn't much, but it was lovingly presented. I had a sudden desire to provide for her, to make sure that she always had food on the table and a warm bed to climb into. It was a domestic side of me that I didn't often feel.

"Okay," she agreed.

"And there's something I'd like to talk to you about," I broke the ice, letting her know that there was an agenda involved.

She regarded me curiously but with a trusting eye that told me she didn't need to hear the details right away. She was up for whatever I needed her to do because she believed in me and she believed in the cause. I would have to take on the responsibility of sending her alone into the lion's den. I wasn't sure if I could do it, but I didn't see another way.

Just then, there was another knock at the door. I froze. I wasn't expecting anyone else and my first thought went to the Angels. Maybe they had come to finish the job and waited until Clara and I were alone together. That was ridiculous, I told myself. The Angels wouldn't knock.

Asking Clara to wait, I opened the door to find my mother and her husband standing on the porch step. They were truly the last people I wanted to see. If it was Simon and his gang I could have gone out, fists flailing. But with Mom, the night was about to take a turn for the worse.

Chapter 8

Clara

I MADE MYSELF SCARCE as soon as Jasper's family interrupted. As I stood up, I glanced down at the takeout food he had arranged on the coffee table. It was a sweet gesture since I knew he wasn't really a homemaker. At least he had found a solid surface for us to eat off of. Often at Jasper's place we ate standing up, huddled around the sink.

Jasper didn't have much furniture in his home. What little he had was limited to the couch and the coffee table. It said a lot to me that he was willing to talk and that he had cleaned up his home in order to play host.

I said hello to Mr. and Mrs. Brown and then excused myself to go to the kitchen. Leaning up against the sink, I tried not to hear them. I pulled out my phone and scrolled through social media. If it had been appropriate, I would have gone upstairs to give them their privacy. But I didn't think either Jasper or his mother would appreciate that. It seemed a little too intimate.

The narrow hallway between the kitchen and the living room did little to disguise their voices, and the argument came through loud and clear.

"What are you doing here?" Jasper said.

"We came to check on you," his mother replied.

"I'm fine, thanks."

"You haven't called or visited since Clay passed," a baritone voice chimed in.

"I didn't call or visit before Clay died either," Jasper snarked.

"It's not fair," Jasper's mother moaned. "It's like I've lost both my sons."

"Don't forget your husband," Jasper warned her.

There was silence, and I felt for all three of the outer room's occupants. I knew they were hurting bad but instead of turning toward each other, they were turning *on* each other. I wished there was something I could do to make it better but I knew it wasn't my place to get involved. Whatever was between Jasper and his parents was none of my business.

"You know I'll always be here for you," Jasper's stepfather said. I could hear the sincerity in his voice from across the room. I didn't know what Jasper had against the guy, except that obviously, he wasn't his real father. It wasn't my place to say anything and I desperately wished for noise cancelling headphones so I could stop eavesdropping. "I just want to support you and your mother through your grieving process," the man continued.

"Because you're not grieving?" Jasper guessed.

"I loved Clay," the man replied, his voice raw.

"I bet," Jasper snapped.

"If you would just let me—" Martin tried. I could hear the desperation in his voice. He had come all this way only to be shut down at the final gate. I knew he cared; I could tell he didn't know what to say or how to say it. But the genuine concern was there.

"No!" Jasper cut him off. "Just get out."

I almost went to them. I wanted to set things right and I could only imagine what Jasper's mom was going through. She had lost one son and the other was so angry with her for remarrying that he wouldn't even let her stay. It was painful to listen to. I turned away to stop myself from running in there.

"Jasper..." the woman sobbed.

"Fuck," Jasper whispered, though the word carried as if it had been shouted. "I'll come visit soon."

"Please do," his mom begged. "That's all that we ask."

"I will. I'm in the middle of something right now," Jasper grumbled.

"Of course," Martin replied.

I heard the door hinges squeak and the sound of feet hitting the porch. A moment later, Jasper walked past me. He reached out for the door to the basement, thundering down the stairs without any explanation. I watched him go, feeling heavy with remorse.

I had just witnessed an intimate family argument, one that no one else should have been privy to. Despite my best efforts at removing myself, I had managed to hear every last word. I didn't know what to do or what to say. Should I just ignore what happened? Should I pretend that his parents hadn't interrupted us and go back to his lovely little dinner on the coffee table?

It seemed like that was probably the best course of action. After what had been said, it was unlikely that he would want to talk about it. I walked into the living room and peeled back the curtain to see Jasper's parents getting in the car. Only they weren't getting in the car just then; they were standing on the front walk, arguing softly.

The window was open and even though they couldn't see me, again, I could hear everything that was said. This time I was culpable. I could have walked away and left them to whisper alone, yet I stayed rooted to the spot because of the magnitude of what they confessed.

"Don't try to act like his father," Jasper's mother said. "Not now."

"But I *am* his father," Martin asserted. "And it's time I told him the truth about it. A man should know who his biological father is."

I wrapped my hand around my mouth to keep myself from gasping. It was a bombshell of epic proportions. Jasper's stepfather, the one he hated with every breath he took, was actually his flesh and blood biological father? How had that happened? What of the man Jasper grew up with? The one who taught him how to ride and fix bikes? Who was that man?

I knew a lot about Jasper's childhood from the time we spent together seven years ago. We were pretty close and we had spent many lazy evenings curled up together talking about old times. I knew that Jasper's father was dead. It was a car accident, which Jasper found ironic because everyone had something to say about how dangerous motorcycles were.

Martin must have moved in during the time Jasper and I spent apart. I didn't know him at all but it was obvious Jasper didn't like him. What crazy twist of fate led to the words I had just heard spoken?

I turned away from the window as soon as I heard footsteps in the kitchen. Jasper returned with two bottles of beer and handed me one. He twisted the cap on his own and drank nearly half of it. I stared at him in unmasked horror, wondering what I was supposed to do.

Should I tell him? It wasn't my secret to tell. I should just keep my mouth shut and let his mother and Martin illuminate him on their own. Yet, knowing what I knew and how hard it would hit him, I had a hard time being firm about that resolution.

"Sorry about that," Jasper said finally.

I stared at my beer, not even sure what to do with it. It was thoughtful of him to share with me, although I didn't really need it. I didn't like the thought that he was drowning his sorrows in alcohol. That path lay nowhere good, but I definitely didn't want to add to his troubles. I couldn't even imagine how he would react.

"I just remembered that I had another case in the basement," he explained.

"I'm sorry," I blurted out. I didn't know what else to say. He was being a good host and helping me transition from the interruption back to our meal. "I can't even imagine what she's going through."

"I can imagine," he said dryly.

I opened my mouth to give him some advice about how to talk to his mother but shut it at the last minute. Who was I to get involved with his family dynamics? It was better for me to just be there for Jasper. He needed a friend right now and that was the best service I could provide.

I tried a smile. He smiled back. "Would you like to eat?"

I looked down at the spread on the table. It was sandwiches from an upscale restaurant, one of the fancier chains across town. Jasper and I had hit them up a few times when we were dating and he knew exactly what I liked. A toasted slab of bread with hummus and roasted red peppers paired with a tiny bag of kettle chips. When I sat down on the couch to eat, my heart wasn't in it. I was just going through the motions.

It was nice that he had thought of me, of us and our relationship. But there were too many things on my mind. I had completely forgotten that Jasper wanted to ask me something. The visit from his parents had mixed up the entire night, making everything seem forced instead of natural.

I tried to be appreciative and I really was hungry. We didn't chit chat as we ate. I kept sneaking glimpses of Jasper over my meal and found him sneaking glimpses of me back. It was as if there were two elephants in the room, one for each of us. I was almost relieved when he finally broke the ice.

There was something he wanted, though if he wanted it for himself or for Clay, I wasn't sure. I shoved my eavesdropping escapade to the back of my mind. It wasn't information I was supposed to have. It could be devastating to my friend and I selfishly didn't want to be the one to tell him. Maybe if I left it long enough, his mother and her husband would find a way to illuminate Jasper. Then I could just swoop in from the sidelines and comfort him.

I put my half-eaten sandwich down on the plate that Jasper had provided and listened to his offer.

Chapter 9

Jasper

I WAS ALL PRIMED TO ask the unthinkable of Clara when my mother and her stupid husband arrived. It took me a few minutes to get back on track. A bottle of liquid relaxation from the basement was just what I needed to hit the reset button.

Clara seemed distracted. I chalked it up to nerves. She was probably still worried about her living situation, so I brought that up.

"How has it been living at home alone?" I asked. "Any problems?"

"I had a security system installed," she said.

"Good," I approved.

"Yeah, it's top of the line. It's costing me a lot. But it has all the bells and whistles. No one can break into my house, and if they do somehow, they can't walk around downstairs without tripping the alarm. There's a panic code for calling the police if all else fails, and there's a computer monitor in my bedroom that shows me everything."

"Everything?"

She blushed. "The downstairs and all around the house outside."

"That's great. I'm glad to hear you're taking precautions."

She sat with that in silence and I didn't know what else to say. We reached a lull in the conversation that I could fill with details about our plan. For some reason, I wasn't ready. I wanted to know more about what she was going through. If I armed myself with knowledge about her mental and physical safety then I would have a better chance of making the right decision.

I was pretty sure she would say yes to whatever I asked. That meant that I had to be triply sure that I wanted her involved. If she got hurt and I was the one who put her in that situation, I would never be able to forgive myself.

We sat in silence, each chewing our own food. There was something else about her that seemed off. She was studying me with an intensity usually reserved for opponents. I sensed that there was something else between us, something that hadn't been there when she arrived. Had my mother's appearance caused Clara to rethink her involvement with my family? Was it worse than I knew?

I tried to focus. Clay's murder demanded an answer and Clara was our best bet. I didn't want to see her hurt but if we could pull it off and get the intel, it would all be worth it. I set down the last of my sandwich, turning to her in earnest.

"Clara," I said. "I have something to ask you."

"Go ahead." She squared her shoulders, prepared for the worst. I wondered what she thought was going on. She certainly didn't seem eager to hear my request. That meant she wasn't anticipating anything good. But had she guessed at my true intent? It might have been obvious, considering the events of the last few weeks.

"Me and the guys were wondering if you would... infiltrate the Angel's Death gang," I spat it out. There was no use being coy. She would understand the full dimensions of our request soon enough. This way, I cut straight to the meat of the sandwich, dispensing with the fluff.

"What?" She sounded shocked, clearly not expecting that sentence.

I continued forward. After diving headfirst into the breach, I was determined to come out the other side. "You spent a few weeks or months dating Simon. He'll trust you."

"He knows that I don't like him. I told him that point blank."

"Walk it back," I suggested.

"How?" she demanded.

"I don't know. Tell him that I made a move on you or something."

She grinned, and I was pleased to see that she still had a sense of humor. She looked even more beautiful when she was smiling and I hated that I had to ask her to do this. I expected her to fall into line, to say that she would follow me to the ends of the earth. I didn't think I would have to argue the point, but her reluctance made me bolder. At least she understood the nature of what we were asking and that it was her choice, not mine.

I wouldn't be railroading her into compliance. She was free to make up her own mind. That meant that if and when she said yes, it would be as a full partner and not as someone who just wanted to help. She was kind but also pragmatic. It relieved me of the burden of responsibility and I was grateful.

Clara turned away, her expression thoughtful. "I don't know. I've just started feeling safe again."

"Think about it," I instructed. "It would be a big help. And we'll protect you."

"Isn't there any other way?"

"Sure," I agreed. "I can go back to Red and Cade and tell them that you said no."

"Don't do that." She held out a hand. "I didn't say no yet."

"We will be there to protect you one hundred percent," I argued. "We won't let you go anywhere without back up. If you're with Simon, one of the Kings or I will be right around the corner. We won't let anything bad happen to you."

"You say that now..." she observed.

"It's a promise," I swore.

She gave an exaggerated sigh. "Okay. How would it work?"

I was actually excited to be moving on from the first stage of the plan. Clara was tentatively on board, so I could share with her the details that the Kings and I had discussed. "You'll give him a call and pretend that something went down between us. You hate the Kings and you hate me."

She laughed softly and I wanted to scoop her up and set her on my lap. It was amazing to see her laughing in the midst of such anxiety. That she had bought an expensive security system didn't escape my notice. Here we were, trying to send her back into the lion's den when she clearly was nervous about ever seeing the Angels again. I wished there was another way, but Red and Cade had made their point effectively. Clara was our best asset to determine who was at fault. Once we had that information, we could yank her out. She would be safe and sound and the Kings could take vengeance against the person or persons who murdered our brothers.

I knew that they felt Clay's death almost as deeply as I did. They were gunning for a chance to wreak havoc. Clay wouldn't have wanted us to retaliate indiscriminately but I had a hard time believing that he would want his own death to go unpunished. Clara was the key and now that she was on board, the game could begin.

"We just need to know who killed Vince and Clay," I told her.

"Only that," she scoffed.

"Make it sound like you hate us. Like you are happy that Clay is dead because that means that I could be next," I instructed.

She leaned back against the couch cushions. Up until that point, she had been perched on the very edge, as if she knew what kind of stains were hidden in the upholstery. With her capitulation, she suddenly didn't care any longer.

"You can say no," I said, not wanting to railroad her.

"I know," she replied. "But you're right. I don't think it would take much effort to convince them that I was on their side. Simon and I had a little bit in common. I do think that he's attracted to me."

"Anybody would be," I said.

She reached out to touch my hand, circling my palm with her fingers. "I'm sorry about what happened to Clay. I want to do everything I can to help you find the guy who did it."

I found myself back at the very beginning. It had taken a lot longer to get there than I imagined, but Clara was willing to put herself in harm's way out of love. Love for me. Love for the Kings. If anyone deserved to be an honorary member, it was Clara. I would put that on the agenda for the next meeting after we decimated the Angels. She had definitely earned a spot in our gang above all the other girlfriends.

I leaned over to kiss her. It was a knee jerk reaction to her astonishing display of bravery. She allowed me to plunder her mouth but I sensed that she was holding something back. Though she threaded her fingers through my hair and stretched sensually beneath me, there was something that she wasn't saying.

I put a hand on her hip, ignoring the lingering doubt. She felt like heaven, her curves so soft I wanted more. She tasted like spice and pepper, the aftereffects of the meal she had just eaten. I let myself fall into the sweetness of her touch. She was my angel, my goddess, the woman who I wanted to be with for the rest of my life.

I was selfish, I knew that from the start. She was going to put her life on the line for me and there was no greater aphrodisiac. Gone was the notion that I shouldn't have been with her that night. There was nothing I could do to disrupt the timeline. If I was with Clay, I might have been laying in a pine box beside him. There was no way of knowing whether I could have changed the outcome of that night.

I thought I had saved Clara that night at Nomad but it turned out that she had probably saved me. Since I was alone with her at the time of the murder, I was able to strike back. We were doing it together and that was the best medicine for grief.

I eased myself away from the sofa cushions, stroking a thumb down her jaw line. Still, she didn't stop me, although I could tell her heart wasn't in it. I reasoned that she was probably nervous about the coming days and that I could unburden her by continuing what I was doing. The only thing I wanted was to make her happy. She meant the world to me and I wanted to show her.

I hooked a finger under her waistband, tugging gently. She was wearing blue jeans and the denim was soft to the touch. She moaned and I knew that I had found her passion. She wanted me just as much as I wanted her. She opened her mouth just a little bit more, fisted her hand in my hair and held on.

I took that as an invitation and helped her onto my lap. She broke the kiss, dropping her hands to my shoulders. Looking down at me, I could see indecision in her gaze. But instead of saying anything, she pressed her lips to mine.

I reached for her thigh, scooting her close. I wanted her to press her chest against me, to give me the all clear to begin removing clothing, but something stopped me. Her advance was hesitant; she wanted it but she didn't want it. I couldn't think of what was wrong other than the fact that I had just asked her to put her life on the line.

I softened my approach. Instead of sliding my hand between her thighs as I wanted to, I rested one on her backside and the other on her shoulder. She meant the world to me and I wanted her to know I would go as fast or as slow as she needed.

The curve of her ass was a dangerous temptation. I wanted to stroke it, to make it come alive with desire. She adjusted herself on my lap and I could feel her engine firing up. She deepened the kiss, rubbing up against me. I thought for sure that this was it. We were going to make love and put all the tension and animosity behind us.

As I moved my hand around to make a play for her chest, she stopped me. Putting her hand against my hand, she held me firm. I looked up into her eyes as she leaned back, breaking the kiss abruptly.

"Is everything okay?" I asked. "If you need more time..."

"It's not that," she whispered.

She stood up, leaving me cold and wanting. I watched her go, my arms dropping uselessly to my sides. She reached for her purse and I couldn't help but admire the curve of her figure. Her hair fell into her face as she crouched to grab the bag from the floor. Raising up to her full height, she slid the strap over her shoulder. I saw the way her chest moved, the way her hips and her stomach were in alignment. I wanted her desperately and I couldn't understand why she was leaving.

"Was it something I said?" I asked.

"No," she replied, shaking her head. "I have to go."

"You don't have to call Simon if you don't want to." I stood up, walking her to the door. I thought maybe she had said yes too quickly and was rethinking her answer. I wanted to let her know that all her options were still on the table; I wouldn't hold her to her promise if she wanted to back away.

"I said I would do it," she replied stubbornly.

Opening the door, she let herself out. I watched her walk across the lawn to her car, which was parked on the curb. She paused at the driver's side door and waved at me. Climbing inside, she sparked the ignition and drove away.

I stared after her in confusion. One moment we had been ready to move the party to my bedroom and the next I was left holding my dick in my hand. What had just happened? I couldn't be sure. Something told me that it had nothing to do with Simon or Clay and everything to do with Clara and me. If that was the case, surely we could have worked things out. She didn't need to rush off like some Cinderella afraid of getting caught after midnight.

I looked around the living room for an explanation. Only our half-eaten sandwiches remained of the evening that had up until recently been going so well. I thought about my mother and her intrusion. Maybe that was the reason for Clara's flight. She had disappeared into the kitchen when we were fighting but it was possible that she had heard something.

Not only was it possible, I chastised myself, but it was likely. There was no door between the kitchen and the living room, only a narrow hallway. Of course, she heard the whole thing and felt bad for me. That was probably why she wasn't turned on.

I didn't know how I was going to make it right, but I knew I had to do something. Relationships were confusing, to say the least. I wished that Clara had stayed and we could have talked about it. Maybe then we could have ended the night more pleasurably. But I had to let her come to me on her own terms. Hopefully there would be another opportunity in the next few days. If one didn't present itself, I would make up an excuse. I didn't just want her as a friend or an honorary King; I wanted her in my bed.

Chapter 10

Clara

I LEFT JASPER'S HOUSE and drove straight home. I forced myself to concentrate on the road. It wouldn't help anyone for me to have an accident because I was distracted while driving. There would be plenty of time to think about everything that had just transpired when I was home with the door locked.

I knew that leaving and arriving were the most dangerous parts of living on my own. I parked in my driveway and reached for a small can of mace I had bought. It was buried deep in my purse, so I had some rummaging around to do. I left the headlights on to discourage any attackers until I managed to locate the weapon.

Turning the car off, I held the can in front of me. I wished that I could test it to make sure that it worked but it felt too dangerous to even try. I didn't know if I would blind myself or if I would create a toxic environment. I just had to trust that the thing wasn't a dud. It seemed like a lot of trust to put into a ten-dollar purchase from a big box store.

Luckily, no one assaulted me between my house and my car. I disabled the alarm and then turned it back on once I was safe and inside. I leaned up against the door, getting no further than my living room.

What had just happened? Things were good between Jasper and me, that much was obvious. He had put the moves on me and was eager to take things even further. If I hadn't interrupted the exchange and fled the scene, I might very well be in his bedroom right now. But I didn't have the stomach to make love, not after what I had witnessed.

How could I sleep with him, knowing the enormity of the secret I was keeping from him?

Jasper's stepfather was his real father. How was that possible? What did it mean for the future of Jasper's relationship with his parents? When did they plan to tell him, or *did* they plan to tell him? I didn't want to be the one to break the news if I didn't have to. Judging by Jasper's comments earlier that night, he wasn't particularly fond of the man. I didn't want to be there when the shit went down. I didn't envy his mother. She was probably torn, not knowing when or how to help her only remaining child come to terms with his heritage.

I put my purse down on the table beside the door. Dropping my keys beside it, I walked into the room. I didn't eat much at Jasper's place even though he had sprung for a meal. I decided to settle my stomach first before going upstairs. It wasn't late and I didn't have anything else planned for the evening.

Investigating the refrigerator, I found some yogurt. I almost ripped the top off before thinking better of it. Why go for the healthy alternative when I had half a tub of ice cream in the freezer? I grabbed a spoon and the pint and sat down on the couch.

The ice cream didn't help calm my racing mind but it tasted sweet and made my stomach happy. I considered what I had agreed to. Getting back into Simon's good graces wouldn't be easy. The way we left things, I seriously thought he might want me dead. Even if he agreed to go out again, would he just be playing me as he had all along? Was there any kernel of desire in his heart or was he as cold as he seemed?

After the fight at Nomad, I had blocked his number. I didn't know if he had tried to get in touch but I doubted it. If he wanted to talk to me, he knew where I lived. Although I had been moving around, first to the hotel and then often at work, so he might have stopped by without my knowledge. Since I couldn't receive calls or texts from him, he wouldn't have any way to alert me to his visit.

I picked up my phone and stared at it. Was I really going to do this? I knew it was important and I was in a unique position to help. It would be difficult to convince Simon that I was really through with Jasper, but it wouldn't be impossible. If I spun the story just right, making it seem like Jasper had tried to take advantage of me, it might work. I could play dumb about the whole Vince and Clay situation, pretending not to know anything about the Angels' murderous habits.

He thought I was stupid once before, maybe he would again. That was more of a possibility than him thinking that I was really in love with him. I would pretend that I didn't want to be alone, that I was through with the Kings and wanted a real man. By insulting Jasper, I thought it was likely that Simon would take the bait.

But even if I could, should I? It would be very dangerous. I was under no illusion that Simon was a pleasant person. He might be the trigger man himself, the one who had killed both Clay and Vince. If that was the case, by opening the door, I would be putting myself directly in the line of fire.

I put the phone down and leaned my head back against the sofa cushions. Another spoonful of ice cream hit the spot and I stabbed at the remote. A goofy movie was what I needed. I would figure out the Clay-Jasper-Simon conundrum later.

I picked a rom-com, one set in New York. It was escapism at its best. The ridiculously beautiful couple got their signals crossed and spent half of the movie in the dark about each other's affections. I got all the way to the first kiss before I turned it off. It was too sappy. I couldn't imagine Jasper and me in the central roles. He would have dispensed with the sexual tension early on, eradicating the plot and moving straight to the happily ever after.

But was that what he was offering? Even if I did this for him and lured Simon into a new tryst, would Jasper forgive me for pulling him away from Clay at that pivotal moment? Would he forgive himself? I didn't want to admit that there were selfish motives behind my agreement to help. I really did care about Clay and I couldn't believe he was gone. Even after a week or more, it seemed unreal.

I didn't see Clay that often so it wasn't his absence that made me grieve. It was the fact that every time I thought about him, I had to remind myself that he had been murdered. And I knew that Jasper was taking it hard. Earlier that evening, I had been surprised to find his home clean. He had appeared relatively sober even though he was drinking throughout the exchange. I couldn't even imagine the pain he was going through. I didn't have any brothers or sisters but knowing that he had grown up with Clay, worked with him, hung out with him, rode in the gang with him, I knew he was feeling the loss every second of every day.

Okay, maybe I was doing it for Jasper and not for Clay, but that was to be expected. Jasper was my one true love. I was sure of it. We had been apart for seven years but I was drawn back into his world on the off chance that he was still available. With the benefit of hindsight, I could see that I had never been really interested in Simon. He was always a stand-in for Jasper.

After rekindling the flame, I had realized that it was Jasper I wanted all along. I thought it was the biking lifestyle and the dangerous men. But I had my heart set on Jasper from the moment I laid eyes on him. It was my ultimate mistake to pick the worst of the worst as a surrogate. Simon was definitely not someone I wanted to associate with. But in order to make it seem realistic, I would have to cozy up to him.

I opened my phone and unblocked him. Then my nerves got the better of me and I blocked him again. I wasn't ready for this. Maybe in the morning I would have more courage. I cleaned up my snack and keyed in the code for bedtime. With two minutes to spare, I hurried upstairs before the motion sensors took effect.

Lying in my bed, I thought I would have trouble sleeping. But all the drama and the anxiety got the better of me, draining my energy. I closed my eyes and next thing I knew, it was morning.

I did feel better. Sleep had given me the clarity I needed to decide what to do about the Kings and the Angels. I would keep Jasper's mother's secret for the time being. I didn't want to interfere in family affairs and it wasn't my place to spill the beans. If there came a time I felt different, I would let him know.

As for Simon, I resolved to give it a shot. I debated what to tell him while I was in the shower. It had to be something realistic. I couldn't just turn on the charm and expect him to swallow the notion that I wanted back into his life. The way we left it, he had basically threatened me several times before starting a bar fight and watching me ride off with the enemy.

I toweled off, imagining where I might be if I was scared of Jasper. I could say that I hid out at a hotel and bought the security system because I was afraid of the Kings instead of the Angels. I forced myself into that headspace before turning the motion sensors off and walking downstairs.

Heaving a great sigh, I unblocked Simon's number and sent him a message. *Can we talk? Something's happened.*

I went to the kitchen to get some breakfast but my stomach wasn't up for it. I turned to coffee instead. It was warm and bitter, the perfect complement to a treacherous phone call. To my great relief, Simon chose to text instead. We had a partial conversation that ended positively. With every ping, my nerves hummed, the anxiety wrapping around my throat like a garrot.

The first thing he sent me was a question mark. That was it. It was a start and it meant that I had his attention. But he wasn't invested enough to spare any words yet. I took a deep breath and began to tell my story.

I'm sorry for running away that night. I wrote. *It was a mistake. Jasper attacked me and I barely got away.*

He considered that for a long time. I stared at my phone waiting for the three dots in a bubble that would indicate he was typing. I almost thought he would call bullshit, but after a few minutes, he responded.

Kings are shit.

I know they are, I agreed.

Now you see why we had to provoke them?

I do. I took a deep breath, following that admission up with a request. *I'd love to see you sometime. I miss you. You were much better than him.* I thought that would get his motor going. Every man wanted to think he was better than the competition.

What are you wearing? he replied. It wasn't an invitation but it wasn't a rejection either.

I almost threw up in my mouth. The last thing I wanted to do was think about Simon in that way. If we got that far again I didn't know what I would do. I couldn't imagine desiring him like that or wanting to feel his hands on my body. He was an awful, massive tyrant. I would prefer to make love to a chainsaw or put my hand on a live wire than ever kiss him again. I stifled my gag reflex and began to flirt. It was one of the hardest things I ever had to do and I knew it was only the beginning. If I played my part right, I would eventually earn another date with the monster.

At that time, I could only hope that Jasper and his friends would be close by, ready to scoop me up if anything bad happened. That was the plan. As awful as it was, I knew it was the only way to get the information we needed. I had to go through the fire to get to the other side.

Chapter 11

Jasper

I KEPT IN CLOSE CONTACT with Clara for several days as she worked her way back into Simon's good graces. Of course, she had to go to work, so she was busy a lot of the time but as soon as she got off, we started texting. We agreed that we couldn't see each other. If the Angels cruised by and saw her car at my place or Clay's bike at her place, the whole plan would fall through. Even going out together was risky. If we were spotted at a restaurant or riding around the city together, Simon would know something was up.

No, it was best to keep our distance. But knowing that she was out there tempting the devil on my behalf was difficult. I wanted to be with her. I wanted to hold her in my arms as she was going to sleep to reassure her that everything would be fine. I was glad that she had spent a small fortune on a security system. It was as much for my peace of mind as for her own.

I made sure to remind her to set the alarm every night. She told me I was worrying too much but I wasn't sure about that. Maybe I wasn't worrying enough. I had, after all, agreed to let her do this thing. I was about to toss her into the snake pit with only a flashlight and a cell phone. It seemed like a grim compromise.

She kept me updated on Simon's texts. She told him that I had attacked her and that she was feeling vulnerable and lonely. She said he was pretty quick to start asking her lurid questions but that he hadn't invited her to go out. I told her to keep it up. The guy was scum and sooner or later he would get tired of imagining her with her clothes off and try to arrange a live showing.

I was right, although half of me wished I wasn't. Soon enough, Clara texted me to say she'd been invited to a barbeque with the entire Angel's Death gang. I hated the idea, but I kept my mouth shut. This was exactly what we wanted. Better, even because it would give Clara a chance to talk to other gang members instead of just Simon.

Not that the Angels would be particularly receptive to questions coming from some random woman, but she might have a chance to eavesdrop on an important conversation. I didn't think that having more enemies would make her safer. Simon was just as likely to try something surrounded by his friends as he was if he got Clara alone.

I had called Red and Cade to let them know that we were on. We agreed to meet at Wheelie's the day before the barbeque, and we were going to take the risk of having Clara there too. They had all promised to be there to protect Clara and I intended to make sure they followed through. If anything seemed off, I was going to pull the plug. We could try again later or come up with another plan that didn't involve my lover. The closer we got to pulling it off, the more nervous I became.

I drove by Clara's house once to scope out the joint. Slowing down, I scanned the street and the adjacent houses for any sign of gang activity. If Simon was there, I could pass it off as stalking behavior. That would be in line with the lies we were feeding him. Thankfully, I didn't see any other motorcycles or anyone I recognized as being related to the Angles. I went around the block and came back, parking in her driveway.

Clara was ready to go, tucking her wallet into her jacket pocket. She gave me a determined smile and though I didn't say anything, I was impressed. She was really going to go through with this. There was no way I could convey my thanks in a meaningful fashion. She was about to give me the one gift that might sooth the anguish my life had become; a chance to avenge my brother's death. It meant the world to me and I hoped we could find a way to make it work. Not at the price of her head though. I wouldn't take it that far.

"How are you doing?" I asked.

"Hanging in there," she said.

We climbed onto the bike, me first and her behind me. She linked her hands around my waist and held on. I felt the gentle pressure of her cheek against my back and realized she was scared. I was scared too, but we were in this together. And we were about to check in with the cavalry.

I pulled out onto the road and sped away, gunning it all the way to Wheelie's. A diner that catered to the biking crowd, Wheelie's was a popular hangout for the Kings. There were other, normal customers who weren't in any gang but we were the one legitimate motorcycle club that claimed the territory.

It had just sort of happened. Clay had started to date one of the waitresses and became friendly with the owner. It was easier for Wheelie's to accept the partnership rather than attempt to cater to multiple gangs. We had made our home there for several years, since before Vince was killed. I felt a sense of familiarity as I pulled up outside and parked in our designated spot.

Inside the diner, we found all the guys waiting. Clay's girlfriend, Jenny, was seated at the table. Clara went right around and gave her a hug. I stayed standing, waiting my turn. She was like family, the closest thing to a sister-in-law I would ever have. She was mourning just like we all were, maybe more so because Clay had been her lover.

There was a lot to discuss, so after offering my condolences, I helped Clara find a seat. Grabbing two chairs from a nearby table, I arranged them side by side. The rest of the guys shuffled their chairs around to make room. Clara sat right beside Jenny and the two women held hands.

I realized anew how difficult this was for Clara. She was going alone into the enemy's camp and all we were offering her was a delayed backup. No matter how close we got to the affair, we couldn't be there with her. She would have to be resourceful and cunning if she was going to make it out in one piece.

I had faith in her but I wanted to make sure our troops got as close to the action as possible. It was time to talk logistics.

"Clara, you know everybody?" I began.

She nodded briefly but I made introductions just in case.

"This is Andrew, Red, Cade, and Al."

"Hello," Clara said.

"She's an Angel," Al said. "I've seen her a couple times with the Reaper."

"That's the point," I replied. "She's been able to use her history with Simon to infiltrate the gang. She got herself invited to a family barbeque and she's going to try to get some intel on who killed Vince and Clay."

"Why should we trust her?" Andrew asked, backing up his friend. It was as if Clara wasn't sitting there along with the rest of us.

"Clara has a long history with Jasper," Jenny spoke up, squeezing Clara's hand. "She's one of us."

Andrew and Al didn't look convinced.

"It was my idea," Cade said.

"It was both our ideas," Red corrected him. "We don't have a better opportunity to get inside the Angels' gang."

"It's true, I went out with Simon a few times," Clara spoke up. "I even thought we were dating for a while, but I never loved him. He was just a person I was with because I missed Jasper."

I looked over at her, hearing her explanation for the first time.

"When Jasper and I broke up it was because I thought I wanted the whole suburban American dream. I thought I didn't want anything to do with any bikers, Kings or Angels. When I came to my senses, Simon was there. He picked me up in a bar and I didn't know how awful he was." She looked at me for confirmation and I encouraged her to continue. "The last few times we went out, he took me to Wheelie's and to Nomad just to provoke you. He knew that Jasper would see us there and was using me to get to him."

"It worked," I said.

Cade grinned. The rest of the gang looked unimpressed.

"The night before Clay died," Clara struggled to continue, being as respectful as possible while explaining her position, "Simon threatened me. He said he knew where I lived and that if I didn't want to suffer the consequences, I would go with him." She looked at me again, her eyes wide and sad. "I was alone and he was there with another Angel. I didn't know what else to do, so I went with him."

"I found Dom trying to choak her out back," I finished the story. "I beat him up pretty good and she came home with me."

"If that's all true," Al said, leaning in, "then how did you convince them to let you back in the gang?"

"I told them that Jasper attacked me," Clara said bravely. "I think he bought it."

"It's the best chance we have," Red added.

"So when's the barbeque?" Cade asked, considering the matter settled.

"Tomorrow," I replied.

"Where is it?" Al asked.

"We don't know," I explained. "But Clara downloaded an app onto her phone that will let me track her. If you all download it too, we can all keep tabs on her. As soon as she's on the move, we'll follow. We'll maintain our distance but stay close enough to swoop in if there's trouble. If all goes well, Clara will be able to learn something about the murders."

"And if all doesn't go well?" Andrew asked.

I looked at Clara. This was the tricky point that I didn't necessarily want to explore. If things didn't go according to plan, there were any number of scenarios we could find ourselves in. Hopefully, a show of force by the Kings would be enough to rescue her. Either that or I could mount a stealth operation and extract her from danger without the Angels becoming aware.

"I've got Jasper on speed dial," Clara answered.

"Worst case, we might be up for another fight," I replied.

"Now you're speaking my language," Andrew said.

Andrew was the youngest gang member and one of the most reckless next to Cade. The two of them would be just fine with a massive frontal assault, although that's what I was hoping to avoid. I didn't want to think of myself as some kind of gang leader. I wasn't. At the moment, we were leaderless and it was more of a congress than a monarchy. I didn't know how to advocate for caution without sounding like I knew better.

"If it comes down to it, we will absolutely fight every last one of them," I said in earnest. "But let's try to get the information first. It's what Clay would have wanted."

"What about Vince?" Al shot back.

He was right. While Clay wouldn't have wanted us to go to jail over a revenge plot, Vince was another matter. He had been a lot more hotheaded than Clay and he probably would have enjoyed knowing that all the Angels were getting a beat down regardless of who had actually pulled the trigger.

"We can beat them all," I agreed. "But let's try to keep the killing to a minimum. If this becomes a massacre, you can be sure the police and the press will be all over it."

The rest of the gang grudgingly agreed. The wholesale slaughter of the Angels would not go over well in the larger community. We would be instantly targeted, arrested, tried, and convicted. We would go down in history as orchestrators of a massacre and that's not what either Vince or Clay would have wanted.

"When it's time, you'll all assemble here," I instructed. "Clara will be at her home and I'll be hidden somewhere close by. As soon as Simon picks her up, we'll start tailing them. When they get to the bar-beque, we'll park somewhere we can remain unseen."

"That is if there's a barbeque," Red observed ominously.

"What do you mean?" Clara asked.

"If they're not on to you," the soldier explained.

Clara looked at me.

I bit my lip in consideration. "What do you think?"

"I think there really is a barbeque," she said slowly. "Although I don't like the alternative."

"We'll be right behind you no matter what happens," I responded.

"Okay," she agreed reluctantly.

The gang split up, having all been given their marching orders. I took my sandwich to go and laid some cash on the table. Helping Clara out of her seat, I took her with me. I didn't have a destination in mind, I just needed to think. Red's comment made me nervous. I hoped that the Angels weren't that smart and that there really was a barbeque.

On the off chance that they were on to us and that we were walking into a trap, I wanted to spend my last moments with the woman of my dreams. I climbed on my bike and waited for her to mount behind me. She slid her arms around my waist and put her cheek down against my back again.

It felt so right, the two of us riding together like that. She was my other half and I had missed her for seven long years. Whatever was in store for us, I hoped we would make it through safely to the other side. I was angry about Clay but if I ended up losing Clara in the process, I would be inconsolable.

I took off into the afternoon, going nowhere. We rode around, just being together, feeling the road beneath us. It was freedom and love at the same time. My heart felt complete. I realized then that I needed Clara in my life and I would do whatever I had to do to protect her. It was a difficult prospect considering what was to come, but I could make it work. Whatever came the next day, I was determined that we would both survive to tell the tale.

Chapter 12

Clara

JASPER ARRIVED EARLY in the morning and hid in the downstairs bathroom. I told him he could come out and watch TV or something but he declined. He stashed his bike halfway down the street, behind a dumpster at an apartment complex. He walked the rest of the way to my door, looking fugitive when I let him in.

He kissed me once before walking straight to the bathroom. He gave me instructions to act as if he wasn't even there. I objected, feeling like he was being overly cautious. As long as he wasn't parked directly out front, I didn't see how Simon was going to know he was there.

"I just don't want to leave you alone with the guy," Jasper remarked, pulling out a magazine.

"You're going to wait there for hours?" I asked suspiciously.

"As long as it takes," he replied.

I closed the door. It was reassuring to have him with me. I knew he was worried about Simon breaking into my house. If the barbeque was a real thing, then it stood to reason there were activities Simon couldn't or wouldn't engage in while we were there. But in my home, without a chaperone, all manner of things became fair game.

I went upstairs to take a shower, brush my teeth, and do my hair. While I was in the middle of the ritual, the doorbell rang. I walked straight to the computer monitor to see who it was. I wasn't expecting Simon for at least another hour.

My heart sang when I saw that it was Zoe. My best friend, whom I hadn't seen since before the fight at Nomad, stood holding a bottle of wine. She didn't have Alice with her, which was good. The last thing I wanted to do was drag a six-year-old into the nightmare that was threatening me and my life.

I hurried downstairs to answer the door, throwing my arms around my friend. She stepped back in surprise, laughing and returning the affection. I hustled her inside, locking the door behind her. She surveyed the living room, her eagle eye missing nothing.

"You got a security system," she said.

"Yeah, well, it's a long story," I replied.

She waited for me to elaborate but I didn't. "Alice and Patrick went golfing," Zoe said finally.

"Golfing?" I laughed. "Don't tell me he's teaching her how to play golf?"

"I'm afraid so," she replied. "I'm going to be a golf mom instead of a soccer mom."

"It suits you."

"I'm not sure if that's a compliment or an insult," she said.

"It's a compliment," I assured her.

"So..." She folded her arms across her chest. "Why the security system?"

"Oh, I was in a bar fight," I responded with more nonchalance than I felt.

"A bar fight?" Zoe gasped.

"Let me get some glasses," I replied, indicating that she should follow me to the kitchen. I picked out two wine glasses and set them on the table.

Zoe uncorked the bottle and poured us each a glass. We sat down to drink, and I caught her up on current events, going into details I hadn't the night I had called to ask if I could stay with her, but still leaving out some of the more objectionable pieces. For example, I didn't tell her that Simon had threatened me or that Dom had tried to choak me. I just said that there was an argument between then Kings and the Angels and that I had left the bar with Jasper.

She gazed at my half-assembled wardrobe and frowned. "Where are you going?"

I looked down at my shirt and blue jeans. I had intended to put a lot of thought into my outfit but being interrupted by Zoe, I just threw something on. I wondered if Jasper could hear us through the bathroom door. I didn't know whether to clue my friend into his presence or not. I didn't know whether to shove her out the door before Simon arrived. I hoped I could keep her safely away from both men and keep her in the dark about what I was really up to.

"I'm going to a barbeque," I said. I figured that was safe enough. It was true and, on the surface, innocent.

"With Jasper?" she guessed, doing a seductive little wiggle.

I wanted to tell her all about my one night with Jasper but I couldn't risk it. Since I didn't know if he could hear, I couldn't be myself. I couldn't talk about him in the way that Zoe would expect me to. She would demand a no-holds-barred down and dirty description of what had transpired and I knew that would make Jasper uncomfortable. Besides, I wasn't going to the barbeque with Jasper so I needed to nip that idea in the bud.

"I'm going with Simon," I said. That was also true although I conveniently left out my true purpose for dating the evil man again.

"I thought you stopped seeing Simon," Zoe objected.

"I did but..." I gazed down at my wine glass, still half full. I needed to come up with a reasonable explanation for my change of heart. "I thought I would give him one last chance."

"I don't like him," Zoe complained.

"He's not that bad," I lied.

"I'm worried about you," she said, taking a sip. "Here you are, hiding away in your own house. You've got a top-of-the-line security system that must have cost a fortune and you're going on a date with the guy who probably spooked you into getting it."

I frowned. She was hitting a little too close to home and it showed. I couldn't meet her eye. I was no good at lying. This didn't bode well for the afternoon's activities, though I was sure it would be easier to fool the Angels than my best friend.

"Okay," I leveled with her, pushing the alcohol away. "There is something going on but I can't tell you what it is."

Zoe chewed her bottom lip for a moment. "Are the police involved?"

"No."

"Should the police be involved?"

"No." I sighed. "Everything is fine. I just need you to trust me."

"Oh shit." She swallowed the rest of her glass in one gulp. "You need to get ready. When is he picking you up?"

I checked my phone. "In about twenty minutes."

"That shirt isn't right. And you don't have any make-up on," Zoe said.

I smiled. I knew I had made the right choice by letting her in even though I hadn't given her any details. She understood that there was some other reason for my date and she trusted me enough to let me go.

We went back upstairs and she fussed with my hair, brushing it out and braiding it behind my back. She dug through my closet and suggested a few shirts. I didn't like any of them. I didn't think that Zoe had a good handle on what a biker would find attractive. All the things she selected were more Patrick's speed than Simon's. We argued and finally agreed on a small black T-shirt. It was technically an undershirt but when I pulled it on, it was concealing enough to wear on its own.

She dabbed a bit of blush on my cheeks and picked out a subtle shade of lipstick. Standing back to admire her work, she gave me the thumbs up. We had just finished when there was another knock at the door.

I checked the screen and saw, to my horror, that it was Simon. This was the first time I had seen him since the fight and I wasn't prepared. Suddenly, the prospect of spending the entire afternoon with him seemed overwhelming. I had promised everyone that I could do it, ignoring the flashing red sirens that were blaring in the back of my mind.

Seeing him on the screen like that was a nightmare come true. Every time I glanced at the monitor, I imagined that very man lurking in the bushes or coming up my driveway. Even though I didn't want to see him, he was there because I asked him to come. He wasn't doing anything illegal.

I wondered if he was the man who murdered Clay. Had he murdered Vince as well? The whole time we were together, had I been kissing and making out with a killer? The thought chilled me to the core.

Zoe read the terror on my face and sobered quickly. "Are you sure you're okay with this?"

I sniffed, touching my hair to make sure it was in place. It was game time. It didn't matter if I was ready for him; Simon was ready for me.

"Come downstairs," I instructed her. "He'll have seen your car in the driveway and it would be strange if you didn't say hi."

Zoe made a face as if that was the last thing she wanted to do. But she followed me downstairs anyway. I thought of Jasper in the bathroom. Hopefully he knew that the chase had begun. Before answering the door, I paused to activate the app. Jasper could track me no matter where I went. It was the only thing I had to make myself feel better as I reached for the doorknob.

Simon didn't look thrilled to see Zoe. I realized too late that it might have been a mistake to let the two see each other. I gave Zoe a quick hug before stepping outside.

"Lock up when you leave," I told her casually.

I knew she was about to be surprised when Jasper came out to follow me but there was nothing to be done about that. I followed Simon to the curb where his bike was parked. Surprising me, he crossed the distance between us in two short steps. I couldn't help a tiny gasp from escaping my lips.

We were in the front yard. No one could help me here, though I thought Zoe might still be watching from the doorway. Simon pulled me in, kissing me roughly before stepping away. I shook my head to clear it, remembering at the last moment to act like I liked it.

I gave him a big smile, doing my best. He favored me with an up and down look and I was pleased that Zoe and I spent so much time picking out my clothes. Without another word, he walked over to his bike and climbed on. I followed, thinking only about Jasper and hoping he hadn't witnessed the kiss. I might be subjected to several of those, or something more intrusive before the day was over. I was prepared for anything. It was all for Clay and for the surviving Kings. I could do this, I told myself.

Wrapping my arms around Simon's waist, I held on tight. But I didn't put my cheek against his back the way I did with Jasper. It wasn't the same. This man I was riding with was the enemy. There was no telling what he might do later that day. As he sped off, I imagined Jasper coming out of the bathroom, running to his bike and giving chase. I just hoped he was fast enough to catch up with us and head off any horrors that might be in store. And I hoped that the barbeque was legitimate. Knowing all that I knew about Simon, I could very well be driving into a trap.

Chapter 13

Jasper

IT WAS IMPORTANT TO me to be close to her, to be right there inside the house just in case that bastard tried anything. But he didn't even step foot in the living room. Instead, she was out the door and down the street before I had time to react.

Coming out of the bathroom, I surprised her friend. There was no time for pleasantries and I didn't even bother to say hello before rushing out the door. It was half a block to my bike and the whole time I was just thinking about how much further away Clara was getting. I knew the rest of the guys were parked close by and that they were probably already in pursuit.

Grabbing the bike – it was Clay's bike but already I was starting to think of it as my own – I gunned it out of the parking lot. Pulling out my phone, I opened the app that would track Clara. To my relief, a bright red dot showed on the screen, alerting me to her position. I took the neighborhood streets out to the boulevard and then to the highway.

I ran into Cade, Red, and the gang on the way out of the city. Falling into the group, I felt stronger. Some of my anxiety over Clara was replaced with determination. We were finally doing something.

Even before Clay was killed, the sensation of helplessness was overwhelming. The Angels kept coming into our spaces, provoking us into fight after fight with no real resolution. They had moved on Clara; they had moved on Wheelie's and Nomad. They acted like they didn't give a fuck and proved there was no way we could protect our own.

At least now we were fighting back. They had no idea what was in store for them. We were going to take down the bastard who was responsible for Vince and Clay's deaths, rough him up, and put him in an early grave. There wouldn't be a massacre, just a quiet retaliation. They would figure it out and they would learn not to mess with us ever again.

Checking my phone, I saw that Clara had pulled off the highway. I signaled to the rest of the crew, lining up to take the next exit. We had to be careful. We didn't want Simon to catch wind of his tail. It would kill the whole deal if he saw the pack of us riding up. I went slowly down the off ramp to give our prey time to drive on. We made up the distance, probably because he wasn't aware he was being followed and was in no hurry.

By the time we came down the ramp and made a right turn onto the country rode, I could see Simon in the distance. We followed as closely as we could without giving ourselves away. He turned left off the main drag and into a space where the digital map said there were no roads. I signaled to my friends to pull back.

We eased off the pavement and into a little wooded enclave. When we turned our engines off, we could hear the enemy's bikes congregating in the distance. It was a good bet that we had arrived at the barbecue location.

I texted Clara to make sure she was okay. Instead of a straight up *Are you okay?* I sent a more cryptic *Do you know where the Miller folder is?* We decided that I would pretend to be someone from work so that she could pass off any communications as innocent. Even if Simon looked at her phone, all he would see was a colleague asking a question about a client.

A moment later, she texted back. *It's on my desk.* That was our code for *everything is okay.* I exhaled in relief. I didn't want to admit that I was worried. There wasn't a high premium placed on love in our world. Women were supposed to be purely recreational, not real people that you got attached to.

Despite that general consensus, both Clay and I had strong feelings for our girlfriends. I guessed it was one more thing we had in common. I wished we had some intel on what was going on over there. Just hearing that Clara was safe for the time being wasn't enough. I wanted to know who she was with, how many of them there were, and what they were doing.

"This is the place?" Cade asked.

I nodded, distracted.

"She's fine," Red told me, picking up on my vibes.

I scowled. I didn't need their pity. I knew they were happy to throw Clara to the wolves if it meant getting information on Clay's killer. I had agreed to the plan and I would play my part. It didn't mean I had to be happy about it.

I stayed glued to my phone, refreshing the screen every time it went dark. We heard some cheering and a couple motors running every now and then. It sounded like a regular barbeque, if such an event could be held by a biker gang. There weren't any gun shots and there were no panicked messages from Clara. Hopefully that meant that she was integrating nicely. Maybe she was even getting the intel we needed.

The guys were all leaning up against their hogs, tossing a pinecone back and forth. No one was drinking. We all knew that it was serious business and that we needed to remain sharp. I was thankful for that. The last thing I needed was to babysit a bunch of drunken slackers while trying to keep my girl safe.

Red kept an eye on me. I could see him checking every few seconds even as he participated in the game. I stood off to one side. I needed my hands free to check and refresh my phone. I didn't want to miss anything.

Clara's red dot stayed put, right in the middle of the field. Every time a cheer went up from the Angel's camp, I got nervous. What if she was in trouble but couldn't get to her phone? I didn't want to chance texting her again. Even Simon would get suspicious with too many work-related communications when Clara was supposed to be off.

I glanced up at the guys and saw that they were having fun. It almost felt normal, pissing the day away in a field far from town. We were comfortable with each other. There was little chatter but some laughter as the pinecone danced from one hand to the next. It felt almost like we were betraying Clay and Vince. I thought it should be a somber event. We should all be glued to our seats, ready to swoop in without a second's hesitation.

We should be focused on the mission, getting the name of the murderer who had dispatched two of our leaders. The relaxed atmosphere was difficult to swallow. I felt like I had a cloud over my head, one that would only dissipate after we achieved our mission. Until then, there was no way I was going to join in the fun.

There was a resurgence of engine sounds and I almost wrote them off. They had been cropping up all afternoon as the Angels presumably rode circles around the barbeque pit. Too late, I realized that the noises were growing louder.

A group of Angels sped past us, abruptly turning and pulling up level to our team. I recognized Theo and Sterling, two of the rival gang members who had fought with us at Nomad. They eased up on the throttle, standing in the middle of the road.

"If it isn't the Kings," Theo called out. "What are you doing here?"

"Lurking in the bushes," Cade answered. He tossed the pinecone over his shoulder and mounted his bike.

We were caught. There was no use trying to hide the fact that we were spying on them. What else would we be doing, pulled over to the side of the road just meters from where the Angels were partying?

"Bet your slow ass bikes can't catch us," Sterling taunted.

Cade didn't answer but lunged into the road, giving chase. Sterling tore away and the two of them raced off into the distance. Theo lingered, his sloppy smile indicating that he was up for some fun.

"Last one to the lake..." the Angel challenged.

Red looked at me and I shrugged. I couldn't very well stick around and pretend that I had business there. Just because they had found our hiding spot didn't mean that Clara was in any trouble. I reasoned that I could just as easily turn around if I got a text. I wouldn't go far.

We all pulled out and dashed away after Cade, determined to beat our rivals. It felt good to have the wind in my face, to be throwing the Angels words back at them as we drove. We were neck and neck for a while, the five of us easily conquering the two of them. Too late, I realized that the distance I was putting between us and the barbeque was the real reason for the distraction. I had left Clara all alone in the hands of the enemy.

Chapter 14

Clara

THE HOUSE SIMON BROUGHT me to was out in the middle of nowhere. There were other homes around, but not within yelling distance. I didn't know if it belonged to a member of the gang or if it was a friend's home they were using for the cookout.

To my great relief, there was a grill set up in the front yard. The land stretched on for acres in all directions but the main plot was trim and the house seemed inviting. Simon pulled up to where all the other bikes were parked and let me off.

Almost immediately, I got a text from Jasper asking if I was okay. I answered him, telling Simon that it was someone from work. He didn't bother to check my phone and that was a good thing. If he was overly suspicious I would have felt more than a little nervous.

There were about a dozen people gathered around. A table near the side of the house had your standard barbecue fare on it; a bowl of chips and two mayonnaise salads. Someone I thought I recognized was working the grill. I could smell the burgers cooking and knew that for the time being at least, I was safe.

There were two other women there as well, making me relax even further. Knowing that I wasn't the only one was a big relief. I left Simon and approached one of the couples to introduce myself. I wasn't under any illusion that the other females would help me out in a jam, but it seemed natural for me to gravitate toward my own sex.

"Hey!" One of the women raised a beer as I approached. She was plump and matronly looking, obviously a wife or a mother, maybe both.

The other woman was a little closer to the house, engaged in a conversation with two big guys. I couldn't let on how pleased I was to see them, so I kept it light. I was supposed to be gathering intel and I knew that whoever this woman was, she probably didn't have the information I was looking for. Still, I was overjoyed to find that this was just a casual gathering and not an execution.

Simon followed me, pulling me against his chest and kissing my ear. I played it off like I was pleased. He didn't bother me too much though, growing bored quickly and searching out the beer.

"Is this your house?" I asked the woman.

"Sure is," she replied. "Mighty nice you could come."

"Thanks," I said with a grin.

I wanted to stick by her so I made up some things to talk about. I asked about her shirt. It was a band T-shirt from several years ago. I told her about a few of the concerts I had been to and we talked music and beer. The biker she was with left and we were alone for a moment. It was the perfect time to see if she knew anything. Just because she was a woman didn't mean she hadn't heard any juicy details.

"What's the deal with the Kings?" I asked. "Simon was just talking about them and it seems like he's really pissed."

"Oh that'll blow over," she assured me. "Just some friendly rivalry."

That was all I needed to hear. Obviously, the woman didn't know anything, or at the very least, she wasn't going to tell me. The rivalry between the Kings and the Angels was anything but friendly. Considering that the Kings were convinced that someone at the barbeque had murdered two of their own, I needed to find someone more knowledgeable about the affair.

"Who's that?" I pointed at the other woman.

"Patty," my new best friend responded. "Hey yo, Patty!" she cried, waving the third woman over.

Patty joined us and together we laughed about some of the guys' idiosyncrasies. I didn't clue them into the fact that I didn't really like Simon. I complained about his riding habits, pretending that they were just adorable little quirks.

Patty had a bruise on her wrist. I caught it when she went to take a sip of her beer. I jumped to the conclusion that her boyfriend gave it to her, but I didn't ask. I didn't know her at all and I wasn't there to investigate domestic violence. Patty was on her own when it came to the Angels. I was only there for one thing.

"One guy I was with before Simon was constantly asking me to bail him out of jail," I lied. It was partially true. I had been with Jasper before Simon, and he did ask me to bail him out once.

"Don't get me started," Patty said, rolling her eyes.

"You don't think they got up to anything more serious than some drunken fights, do you?" I asked conspiratorially.

"No," the first woman scoffed.

Patty held her tongue and I could see she knew something more that she didn't want to share. Was she aware of the murderous activities of the gang? Could she provide the information I was seeking?

I was about to come up with yet another probing question, when I heard Simon's voice behind me. Turning to look, I saw that he was standing in a group of four men, just a few feet away. They were all drinking and it looked like Simon had already ingested more than one. Just the way he was standing, leaning slightly to the left, and the way his mouth crooked up when he spoke indicated that he was well on his way to being drunk.

That didn't bode well. Not only was he my ride home but he was infinitely more dangerous when he was trashed. I didn't want to be alone with him to begin with, but the sight of him getting plastered turned me off even more.

I looked back at the women and they knew what I was thinking. Thank goodness it wasn't an inappropriate response. Patty leaned close and whispered, "They're all getting drunk. Looks like we better do the same."

I laughed. I definitely didn't want to follow suit. I needed all my faculties to get the information and stay safe. But I could see that alcohol was a way of coping for these women. It was probably easier to deal with their abusive husbands and boyfriends if they were already blunted to reality.

As we were standing there, joking with each other, I heard someone mention the Kings of Hades behind me. Very delicately, I swung my head around to glance in their direction. It was Davy, that bastard who had threatened me with horrible things at Nomad just before the fight. I hated him even more than I hated Simon.

He was the leader of the Angel's Death gang and a perfect source of information. Whatever went down and whoever was to blame, Davy would know all about it. I listened in, flicking a switch in my inner ear to focus in on the conversation behind me. I did my best to engage in both things at once, pretending to listen to what Patty was saying while I was really only interested in Davy.

"The Kings lost another leader," Davy was saying.

There was some snickering and a general sound of approval from the gang members gathered around. I wanted to punch them all. I wanted to rip off the mask that I was wearing, the one that marked me as an Angels sympathizer, and reveal myself as Jasper's girlfriend. How dare they insult Clay's memory by laughing about his murder?

Yet Davy didn't seem to be disrespectful. He raised his beer and proposed a toast. "To Clay Ayers and Vince Marsh. May they ride forever."

"Ride forever," some of the other bikers agreed.

I glanced over at Simon and saw him smirking. I wondered what it all meant. Was Simon the one who had pulled the trigger? Had I unknowingly fallen in with a murderer? Was Davy in the dark about what happened? Was his toast sincere? If Davy really thought he was honoring the fallen leaders of the Kings, but Simon was the one who had put them in the ground, what did that say about the Angels? Maybe there was more going on than met the eye.

I had been assuming that they were all in it together. A lot of the Kings felt that way. I knew I was supposed to figure out who among the group was personally culpable but I hadn't expected to find them so fractured. If one of them did it, I expected the others to know. Davy's show of camaraderie with Clay took me by surprise and left me uncertain how to continue.

Simon left the group of guys and came toward me. I held my breath, trying to psyche myself up for the acting that I would have to do. Every time I thought I couldn't get more disgusted with him, he proved me wrong. Knowing that his fellow Angels were celebrating Clay's life while Simon just smirked made my stomach turn. I didn't know how I was going to continue pretending that I liked him.

Just then there was a commotion and the sound of bikes driving by on the road. The entire party looked over to see Jasper, Red, and the rest of the Kings riding by. I noticed there were a couple others, maybe members of the rival gang. My heart sank, knowing that was my entire protective detail riding off into the distance.

Simon followed my gaze as did everyone in the party. There was no missing the show of force demonstrated by the more than half dozen bikes riding past. I held my breath, wishing I could disappear. How reckless did Jasper and his friends have to be to ride past the party they were supposed to be stalking?

I tried not to let the dismay show on my face. I tried to look as surprised as everyone else. But Simon latched on to me. He wrapped a hand around my arm and tugged. "What the hell are *they* doing here?"

"I don't know," I said. He was holding me tightly enough to cause pain but I didn't allow myself to squirm. I set my jaw and stuck to my line. "Maybe they're following me."

"Maybe you're working with them," he surmised. "Are you a spy?"

"No." I pulled back against him, desperate to free myself.

"How else would they know we're here," he snapped, pulling me close so I could see his ugly teeth.

"Let me go," I complained.

"Let her go," Davy said, waving his beer around. He was three sheets to the wind and less of a champion than I needed. But Jasper was gone and Simon was determined to shake a confession out of me. I had to take help where I could find it and the drunken leader of the Angels was as good a place as any.

Simon released me. He might know something about Clay that Davy didn't know but then again he might not. Either way, he wasn't ready to disobey a direct order just yet. It worked to my advantage. I muttered something about needing to use the bathroom and hurried to the house.

Going in through the front door, I found myself in a comfy little living room. The sofa and chairs were bright orange and a colorful rug covered the floor. If I wasn't in the company of murderers, I might have been lulled into a false sense of security. As it was, no amount of cheerful furnishings could put my mind at ease. I hurried to the nearest door, finding a bathroom, just as I had hoped.

I locked the door but the deadbolt was barely hanging on by a thread. It might hold the door shut against innocent people but if someone wanted to get me, a single kick would bring the thing crashing open. I put my back against it to provide some amount of strength. Pulling my phone out, I called Jasper.

He was supposed to be just a phone call away but when I needed him the most, he didn't answer. The call went straight to voicemail and I couldn't think of any message colorful enough to leave. I couldn't believe he had talked me into this and then left me hanging at exactly the wrong moment. I had a few choice words I wanted to share with him and the rest of the Kings. The only problem was that I was trapped with Simon all alone and I would have to talk my way out.

My heart was beating wildly. I rushed to the sink to splash some water on my face. The only thing I had going for me was myself and my wits. Simon might be a killer and Davy might be in the dark but I knew what was going on. It was up to me and me alone to get out of the barbeque alive. I didn't know what the hell I was going to do but I had to figure it out fast.

Cursing Jasper and Simon in the same breath, I prepared myself to go back out into the fray. I couldn't stall forever, even though I really wanted to. I felt the weight of the world resting on my shoulders but it was really just the weight of my own life. The next few moments were all I had between me and certain death. I had to spend them wisely.

Chapter 15

Jasper

IT WAS STUPID BUT I didn't care. It felt good to speed down the road, catching up to the Angels and passing them. I leaned heavily on the throttle, pushing Clay's bike to the limit. It was a new ride for me and I was still learning its quirks. It surprised me by inching its way past seventy then eighty then ninety miles per hour. Clay was a maniac with a wrench, it seemed.

One wrong turn and I would be a stain on the roadway but that was just what I needed to feel like a real person again. I forgot all about Clara and the vigil I was supposed to be keeping. The desire to beat the rival gang was the only thing that mattered.

Without even knowing it, we thundered past the gathering. Too late, I realized that I recognized some of the people standing in the front yard. They all held drinks and were congregating around a grill with plates and burgers. I saw Davy's face as I sped past and belatedly spotted Clara among a small group of women.

It was too late to turn back and acknowledging them would only make it worse. If I recognized them there was a good chance they had recognized us. The fact that Clara might find herself in danger or that the Angels might be motivated to give chase didn't occur to me. I was drunk off the speed and the power of my ride. I was focused on achieving the ends of our race, to win against Theo and Sterling.

The wind whipped my hair against my face. The pavement blurred beneath me. I poured all my energy into the chase. It was brilliant and maddening at the same time. I could see my life in perspective. All the fights with the Angels and the struggle for dominance in Stroudville suddenly seemed crystal clear.

My life was here among my brothers. There might be other things going on in the world, politics and war, but none of that could touch me. What was important was my gang, my city, and the ghosts that haunted me. I was only a small piece of a larger puzzle. This was my responsibility, getting revenge for Vince and Clay and making sure that none of the rest of us fell victim to the killer.

We followed the road past another half dozen houses until it broke out into corn fields. Theo took a dive around a steep turn and spilled into the field. I slammed on the brakes, ready to announce my victory. Coming back to where he fell, I couldn't help laughing.

The man was fine. He might have torn up his leg but he was walking. His pants were scuffed by not torn which probably meant there was no bleeding or serious injuries. Theo limped back to his bike, righting it, and walking it back to the road.

Suddenly, I didn't feel so angry with them. Sterling coasted up to us, sandwiched by Red and Cade. We were all just people, just bikers enjoying the road. The adrenaline from the chase thundered through my veins, making me high. I felt like an overgrown kid, someone who had just won the big game and was ready to celebrate with his friends.

It took me a minute to remember that Theo and Sterling were sworn enemies. There wasn't anything innocent about what we were doing. We were there to investigate whether they had killed my brother, not to figure out who stole the school's mascot. We weren't kids. If I met these two at Nomad or at Wheelie's, we would be pounding on each other with a vengeance.

I looked back at Red and Cade to see how they were reacting. They were each grinning, pleased that the Kings were faster than our rivals. It seemed that everyone was swept up in the moment and no one was thinking about the consequences.

I remembered seeing Clara at the party as we drove past and dove for my phone. In my exuberance for the chase, I had completely ignored my post. We were supposed to be protecting Clara. She put her life on the line for us and we abandoned her. I was the worst, because I actually cared about her. Red and Cade could care less. But I should have stood my ground, remained nailed to my phone screen and resisted the temptation to race.

I saw that there were two missed calls and several texts from Clara. Cursing myself for being so short sighted, I opened the texting app to read the messages. The first one was from a few minutes ago. She was panicking.

Simon is suspicious. Why did you leave me?

I felt a stab of guilt as sharp as any wicked instrument. Hurrying on to the next text, I saw that she was still alive. She was angry, as well she should be.

Dammit! Where are you?

She must have found a way to text me even though there were other people around because the next sentence was a warning.

They're coming for you. All of them.

"The Angels are on their way," I told the Kings.

We were all collected by the side of the road, lording our win over Theo and Sterling. But the Angels were on their way. If we stayed, we were sitting ducks. I almost wanted the fight. It wasn't what we came for but it would have been satisfying to feel my fists connecting with Simon's or Davy's face.

We were no closer to figuring out who killed Clay or Vince, unless Clara was holding back. It was one of them, one of the bastards who were on their way to our location. If I just held my ground, I would come face to face with the lot of them. We could bury the hatchet in their ugly faces, expending all our aggressive energy in one final confrontation.

I saw that Red and Cade were also tempted to stay. Al and Andrew seemed like they would be up for it. Theo stuck his chin out and gave us an evil grin, knowing that his friends were on their way.

"You better run," Sterling said. He was sore over the loss and it showed.

"And if we don't?" Cade snarled. "Maybe we should start the fight right now." He stepped toward the Angel, spooking him with a raised fist.

Sterling flinched. It wasn't a good look and the Kings laughed. The Angels were a bunch of pussies and everyone knew it. Clay might have found himself alone in a gang fight but I had no doubt that he went down swinging. Sterling looked like he might run or maybe even cry. I felt powerful, connected to all my friends and capable of ending the rivalry right then.

"There are more of us than there are of you," Sterling said, clutching his handlebars tight.

I looked at Red. He was the most responsible of all of us. While we didn't have a leader, I knew everyone would follow his lead. He glanced around the circle, making eye contact with each of us. Finally, he tilted his head toward the road.

"Let's go."

"You better run," Sterling cried.

"We'll be outnumbered," Red argued. "We're going to lose if we stay."

Cade snarled, tearing off down the street without another word. I knew he wanted to fight. He was the hothead among us, the one who was chomping at the bit to get back at the Angels. If he was willing to leave, the rest of us had better be close behind.

I took off, feeling the slip of air as Al and Andrew passed me. Red took up the rear and together we peeled away, leaving Clara on her own. The operation was a complete trainwreck. We had gained nothing and stood to lose everything. A moment of fun turned what could have been a successful mission into a failure. I felt the guilt well up in my heart until it flooded my eyes and tore through my brain. If anything happened to Clara now, it would be my fault. I could only hope she would be okay. There would be two Ayers in the ground instead of one if she suffered. If anything bad happened, I didn't think I could live with myself.

Chapter 16

Clara

AS SOON AS I CAME OUT of the bathroom, Simon found me. He wasn't fooled. He knew something was up and that I was in the middle of it. I tried to play it off like I was just as surprised to see Jasper and the Kings as he was but it wasn't working.

"Stay here," he snarled, grabbing my arm again.

I set my jaw, determined to stick up for myself. He might be bigger and stronger than I was, he might have experience beating a man to death, but that didn't mean I had to act scared. If it was my time to die, then so be it. I wasn't going to beg him to leave me alone. I would kick and scream and bite, whatever it took to free myself.

Luckily, none of that was necessary. All the guys were getting on their bikes to follow the Kings. Simon released me and stalked over to his motorcycle. He took off after his rivals, leaving me alone with the women and one older guy. I gazed at them momentarily before walking down the driveway.

Since the cavalry was gone and I was on my own, I couldn't see that I had another choice. It was either hang out among the enemy and wait for Simon to come back and attack me or run away. Since I didn't have my own bike or my car with me, the only method of transportation available was my feet.

I turned right where all the guys had turned left. Hopefully Jasper would be able to keep the Angels busy for long enough. I thought I re-membered passing a convenience store not too far down the road. If I could make it there, maybe I could call a rideshare.

There were no sidewalks and the space between houses was enormous. I walked for at least three minutes before the next driveway and another five minutes until the one after that. The sun beat down, warming me from above. It was a nice day. Too bad I was trying to escape from a murderous biker gang, otherwise it might have been a nice walk.

I passed a few mailboxes and then there was nothing, just trees and grass. I was starting to think that the convenience store was just a mirage when I heard the distinct sound of a motorcycle coming up behind me.

There was nowhere to run. I couldn't take off into a field, I would be chased down in a matter of minutes. I couldn't run along the road because I wouldn't get very far. It was past the time that I could hide; whoever it was had already seen me.

I had a flash of terror, thinking it was Simon. He had come to collect me, to punish me for bringing the Kings to the barbeque. Or maybe it was another Angel, equally suspicious. They would scoop me up and drag me back to the scene of the crime. I would be forced to answer for things that I had no knowledge of and left for dead by the side of the road.

But when I turned, I found the one person that I longed to see. Jasper rode up behind me, slowing to a crawl so that I could get on. Without complaint, I threw my leg over, climbing onto the bike. I wrapped my arms around his waist, pulling him close. Laying my cheek against his leather jacket, I felt like I was coming home. I was safe at last and the nightmare of the barbeque was over. I didn't have to pretend any longer. I hadn't learned anything valuable, except perhaps that Davy didn't know everything.

Was that bit of knowledge worth blowing my cover? Simon wasn't going to invite me to any more of the Angels' gatherings. It had been risky at the start but it had become too dangerous. The way he looked at me before driving off told me everything I needed to know. No amount of protesting on my part would bring him back around. He was convinced that I was working with the Kings and he was right. I wasn't angry with Jasper even though he had left me at the party. I was just relieved that he found me.

Together, we rode away from the chaos back to my place. I hadn't seen anything so welcome as my own home in a long time. The thought of getting inside and turning on the security system was heaven. I wanted to bury my head in the sand, to forget about the biker feud and the murders for the time being.

Jasper came with me. I didn't invite him in but he must have known I didn't want to be alone. I was grateful for his company and searched for a beer in the refrigerator to offer him, but didn't have any.

"I'm sorry, I don't have any beer," I said.

"That's okay."

He stood in the living room awkwardly, not wanting to leave. I took a seat on the couch and patted the cushion next to me. He sat down, relieved. It might not be the satisfying resolution we were looking for, but we were both safe and together for the moment.

"Why did you leave me at the picnic?" I asked, needing to know.

"I'm sorry," he responded. "Things got out of hand."

"Did they catch up to you?"

"We split up. I don't know what happened to the other guys. I came back to get you."

And there it was; the perfect sentence. It didn't matter what came before, what mistakes had been made or how high the stakes were. Jasper came back for me. He didn't leave me in the enemy camp; he left his fellow bikers to come find me. I laid my head down against his shoulder, relaxing for the first time in hours.

He put a hand on top of my head, stroking my hair. It was a friendly gesture, but I was sure there was more to come. It was still light out and though the barbeque was meant to serve as dinner, I hadn't eaten anything yet. Food wasn't on my mind, though. There was a different hunger growing in my belly.

I turned my face toward Jasper and found him thinking the same thing. Our lips connected and I closed my eyes. The feel of him so familiar beside me was wonderful. His beard scratched my cheeks, making me long for more. He was the perfect man, solid and protective but just a little bit dangerous. I could lie there in his arms all day, basking in the warmth of his touch.

His jacket crinkled as he gathered me near, its leather smooth on the outside and warm underneath. I slid my hand up the side of his body, beginning at his abdomen and ending on his shoulder blade. He was every bit as hard as I remembered, a perfect sculpted figure beneath layers of discontent.

He pulled the jacket off, lying it down on the couch beside him. Wearing just a T-shirt, he turned back to me, resuming the kiss. I broke it off a moment later with a wicked idea. I felt dusty after walking down the road in the hot sun. A shower would hit the spot, but a shower with Jasper would be even better. I didn't know how to lure him in with me so I decided to just ask.

"Do you want to take a shower?"

He looked down at me and grinned. It was the first time I saw him smile since Clay died and it warmed my soul. I wanted to give him everything I had, to wrap him up in a love so strong it could heal all wounds. My heart was a gift I could give to him. It was all that I had but it was more than enough.

Eagerly, he nodded, licking his lips in anticipation. There were two full baths in my house but somehow the one upstairs seemed the most appropriate for our purposes. I stood up off the couch, intending to walk to the stairs. But Jasper lunged at me, circling my waist with his powerful arms.

I laughed, working my way free and racing to the second floor. I felt free, as if all the cares in the world couldn't bother me. We were alone, standing on the precipice of the future with every possibility open before us. I couldn't imagine anyone I would rather be with at that moment. Jasper was my best friend, my partner in crime, and I was about to take him again as my lover.

I darted into the bathroom, leaving the door open for him to come inside. He followed me without delay, pulling his shirt off so I could see his spectacular abs. Tossing the garment into the corner, he pushed the door closed. I knew I had only seconds until he was on me, so I twisted the shower dial to start the water. It had to heat up just like we did or else we ran the risk of an icy encounter instead of a steamy affair.

Jasper pounced a second later, pushing me up against the wall. He took my wrists in both hands and nailed them to the surface above my head. I moaned softly. I loved the rough play. It was why I had abandoned the idea of a comfortable home in the suburbs. No nine to five man could give me what I wanted.

He kissed me roughly, all pretenses gone by the wayside. I inhaled, seeking that one last breath of fresh air before taking the plunge. The sound of the shower drowned out my final protest as I gave myself fully to the man I loved.

He pressed his body against me, cutting off all avenues of escape. I didn't want it to end. I wanted more and tore into the embrace with a hunger that startled me. Caught between the wall in back of me and the solid body in front, I lengthened my torso. Rising up on my toes, I sought to even the playing field. I didn't want to be some helpless woman ravaged by a starving man. I was an equal partner in the game.

He closed his mouth, sealing the kiss and moving on to my ear. Sucking the lobe between his teeth, he nibbled gently. He kept one hand on my wrists but moved the other to my breast. It was happening so quickly. One moment we were lounging together as friends and the next we were engaged in the most erotic of dances.

I felt myself falling backward, falling into my dreams. It was as if the wall became a bed and we were writhing on top of it. I longed to stroke his beard, to run my fingers through his hair and pull him close. But he denied me that pleasure, taking his time, encouraging me to submit.

His palm grazed my nipple, his touch deep and insistent. Steam began to rise from the shower stall, indicating that the water was ready. I didn't care at the moment. We might make love right there next to the toilet for all I cared. It was dirty and devious but somehow clean at the same time.

We were about to take the plunge together, waylaid on the shore for a long moment. He broke away to reach for my shirt and I took the opportunity. As soon as he released my hands, I was all over him. I allowed him to lift the garment from my skin, to slide it up over my arms and cast it away. But that was the extent of my charity.

I gathered him to me, raking my fingers down his back. The swell of muscle beneath his skin was enticing. I couldn't wait to feel him completely nude. Sliding one palm down his spine, I dipped into his pants to cup his buttock. He pressed a knee between my thighs, rubbing my most intimate space as he shoved me back into the wall.

I had lost my opportunity. I couldn't reach between us to undo his fly so I had to content myself with a handful of his ass. It was hard and smooth, a perfect metaphor for what was to come.

After a moment, he decided that the clothes were too obtrusive. He let me go, reaching for his own clasp. I took note, pulling my jeans off and casting them aside. By the time I was done, he had shed his own pants, kicking them into the corner with the rest of our items. Only our underwear remained to block us from indulging and we made quick work of that.

I hopped in the shower before he could stop me, cupping my hands to collect the warm water. It was heaven. After the stress of the party, I was ready to lose myself to delicious sensations. I ducked my head into the stream, feeling heat sluice down my neck and past my chest.

He was with me in an instant, caring nothing for the rain, his entire being focused on my body. The brutality of the past few minutes was gone, replaced by a tender longing that made my skin burn even hotter. He closed his mouth over mine, tilting my chin up so that he could have access.

The water streamed between us, stealing my breath and intensifying the action. He guided me to the wall, our feet trapped in the gentle, sloping tub. His hands started at my neck, cradling the skin where Dom had attempted to choak the life out of me. Lingering only a second, he trailed his fingers down past my shoulders to my elbows before making the leap to my waist.

Blindly, I reached up to the nozzle for the bodywash that dangled in a caddy. Looping my arms around his neck, I squirted scented liquid across his shoulders before replacing the bottle in its carrier. Soaping his back, I luxuriated in the feel of lubricated skin. I traced soapy circles around his shoulder blades, down the slope of his spine to his back side.

He slid his knee against my crotch again, this time touching my core. I reveled in the contact, opening myself up to the intrusion. He was warm and wet, growing hard down below. I rubbed my soap-covered hands across his hips, discovering that there was no soft flesh on his body. He was a mountain sculpted from marble, a living statue that must have taken hours to define each day in the gym.

I was able to slip one hand between us, searching out the definition of his manhood. He wasn't stiff yet but well on his way. I closed my fingers around the base, lovingly coaxing him to life.

He took a fistful of my hair and pulled down, forcing me to look up. I closed my eyes, surrendering to the call. I felt his tongue circle my nipple before he closed in to suck at my breast. I could still feel him in my palm, the soap a foamy residue between us. I pulled incessantly, urging him on.

He dropped his hand from my hair and reached around to grasp me by the ass. I struggled to right myself, leaning forward as he hauled me into his arms. Drunk with pleasure, I bit into his shoulder, tasting clean water and just beneath it, sweat and leather.

He pushed my spine against the wall, centering my crotch around his hips. I felt the sting as he slid his cock inside, pushing past all my barriers to lock himself deep within. The intrusion was staggering. I dug my fingernails into his biceps, fighting against the emotion that threatened to consume me. He was so big and I felt helpless in his arms. He was a warlord, a titan and I was his mistress.

I wrapped my legs around him and held on tight. He kept one hand on my thigh, holding me steady as he began to pump. Everything else in my life faded away. Simon didn't exist and I couldn't remember my own name. My work, my home, all the fear and anxiety drifted away, pushed to the back of my mind.

I was one with the man inside me, taking pleasure from every stroke. He beat me senseless with his massive rod, teasing me higher and higher until I didn't think I could take it anymore.

I cried out. "Jasper!"

He paused in his wicked pursuit, thrusting deep. "Clara."

"Jasper!" I screamed again, grabbing fistfuls of his hair, begging him to continue.

He heard my plea and got down to business, dragging his cock in and out of my soul. I gasped, watching the world go dark before fireworks exploded all around us. Blood thrummed through my core, pulsing out a rhythm that was unmistakable.

He felt the change within me and ended his own journey in three quick strokes, pressing me against the wall, covering my body with his own. He was so deep, I could feel him unload his burden in the very center of my being. I exhaled in relief, dropping my head down onto his shoulder. It was over but it was only just beginning. With that single act, we destroyed every last remaining doubt between us. We were joined at the hip, consumed by our mutual attraction. He was my man and I was his woman. No matter what happened, we would face it together.

Our hearts beat together, pounding against each other from separate rib cages. I gathered him to me as my breathing slowed, exhausted but already aching for more. He set me down, withdrawing slowly from my core.

He kissed me feverishly, sliding a thumb down my jaw. Having expended our nervous energy, we spent the rest of the shower washing each other off. I grabbed a handful of soap and smoothed it down his back, careful to trace all the ridges and outlines of various muscle groups.

He lathered me up, spending an inordinate amount of time caressing my breasts and hips. We fondled each other to arousal again, but got out of the shower. My skin was starting to prune and once standing up was enough. We raced across the hallway to my bedroom and locked lips again, sliding beneath the covers.

All the excitement at the barbeque had both of us on edge. Fucking our way to salvation was the best way to leave it all behind. I fell asleep, boneless and exhausted, his arm around my stomach. For the moment, at least, I felt safe and well loved. Unfortunately, it didn't last.

Chapter 17

Jasper

I ROSE TO CONSCIOUSNESS in Clara's bed. The night before was hot and heavy and sorely needed after the week I'd had. Delving into her private spaces took the pain away and it felt like a lifetime since I was able to put it all aside. I lapped it up like a greedy puppy, intent on bringing myself to orgasm as many times as possible.

We had fallen asleep together, naked as the day we were born. She felt right in my arms, her lithe form snuggled up against me. I cupped her breast as if there was still some unfinished business between us, but when I woke up, I wasn't in the mood.

I drifted out of a nightmare that felt so real, it shook me. In it, Clay was lying in the morgue, looking up at me with an accusing eye. The other one was blasted out of his skull and the gaping hole was just as angry.

I took a step back, not understanding. It was then that I remembered my guilt and the fact that I had likely been screwing Clara when he died. *How dare you fall back into her arms?* He screamed silently. *Haven't you done enough to hurt me?*

I plowed my way up through layers of sleep like invisible netting, holding me down. My body twitched as I came back to life, as if I was some monster being shocked awake. I pulled Clara close to me before I realized what I was doing.

Shame crept up on me. I couldn't believe I had fallen for her charms again. What was I doing? I should be singularly focused on getting revenge, not wallowing in love. Love couldn't bring Clay back. The only thing that mattered was making someone pay. I couldn't afford to play nice or to sleep over.

I got to my feet, crossing the room to search for my clothing. With a wicked grin, I remembered that they were in the bathroom. I had spent most of the previous night without a stich of fabric and no matter how much I wanted to regret it, I didn't.

Clara stirred. I had hoped to get out of there without waking her but she sat up, alarmed. Her eyes narrowed just as my hand reached for the door. I knew I was caught.

"What are you doing?" she asked.

"Getting my clothes," I replied.

"Are you leaving me?" she demanded.

I turned back to her, wanting to put an end to it but unable to find the words. She looked so hurt and I didn't want to be the one hurting her. Memories of the night before came back to me; all the positions we had used and the way her body felt beneath mine. It wasn't right. Whatever I needed to do to satisfy Clay's angry spirit would have to wait.

"No," I lied. "I was just going to get breakfast."

"I'll come with you," she said.

I agreed with a smile and snuck across the hallway to get my clothes. Standing in the bathroom, getting dressed, I worried about my state of mind. The previous night I had spent drinking alone and now I was playing house with Clara. I thought I should be stoic, I should drown my sorrows as any righteous biker would do, in a bottle and not in a beautiful woman. But Clara was a thousand times better for my heart than any drink.

I might not be the perfect revenge soldier. I might not live a lifestyle dedicated to my fallen brother, but the thought of walling myself off from Clara was too painful. She was important too. It wasn't just bikers in the world. She valiantly threw herself into the line of fire for me and for the memory of Clay, and I couldn't forget that.

After I dressed, I picked up her clothes and took them back to her room. She was out of bed and halfway decent by the time I arrived. I kissed her good morning without regard to morning breath. She relaxed in my arms and I realized she was worried that I would sneak away without saying another word. It hurt that she thought so little of me but I knew I deserved it. In the past I had done such a thing, leaving her after screwing her. She was only reacting to the pattern she knew. And I had been planning to do the exact same thing before she stopped me.

With an angry snarl, I broke the kiss. I was angry with myself, not with her. Vince may have demanded a single-minded pursuit of revenge but Clay wouldn't. Clay would want me to find love and happiness in Clara's arms. He would be livid if I threw it all away to chase the dreams of a dead man.

"Is everything okay?" Clara asked.

"No," I grumbled. "I'm just thinking what an ass I've been."

She smiled, following me out into the hall and down the stairs. "I won't argue with that. But you've had one hell of a month."

"So have you," I reminded her.

She put a hand on my shoulder in solidarity and I placed a palm over it. I knew I would win a horrible month contest but she deserved some recognition as well. She had been attacked by Dom at Nomad and threatened by Simon. I continued to keep her off balance, not intentionally, but that's just how it worked out. And she was likely grieving Clay in her own way. They were friends and they knew each other from way back.

We broke into the kitchen and Clara told me to sit. I liked it when she was bossy, so I followed her orders. She grabbed a box of oatmeal from the cabinet and a jug of milk from the fridge. I watched her backside as she prepared the meal and she caught me looking.

"Eyes up here," she teased, indicating her face.

"You were looking at the stove," I replied.

She pressed her lips together, returning to her task. As she filled up the coffee pot and emptied the water into the reservoir, I remembered what we were supposed to be doing. Clara had spent several hours with the Angels the day before. Even though I messed it up by acting like a fool, she might have learned something.

"Were you able to find out anything at the picnic?"

"Not really," she answered, sliding a bowl in front of me.

She grabbed two spoons and stuck them in the mush; one in my bowl and one in hers. Grabbing two coffee cups, she filled them to the brim with heated brew, setting them one by one on the table.

"There was something that I wasn't expecting," she mused, taking a seat beside me.

I watched her taste her oatmeal first, then her coffee. She seemed to be in no hurry to finish her statement. I waited patiently, even though I felt like I might burst. To pass the time, I tried my own breakfast and found that it was good. Maple brown sugar or some other overly sweet flavor infused the oatmeal and made it tolerable.

"Davy gave a toast to Vince and Clay and it seemed sincere," Clara said finally. "It sounded really heartfelt. He wasn't making fun of them and most of the Angels were right there with him. It was just Simon. He had this look on his face when Davy was trying to honor your gang leaders, like a smirk. I think if anybody killed Clay it was Simon. And I'm not sure that Davy knows about it."

That was some good intel. I leaned back in my chair, stroking my beard. For a moment, I didn't know what to say. All along, I had assumed that everyone in the Angels gang had been in on the crimes. Davy was the leader. If he was genuine in his sympathy for the Kings then we were talking about a rogue agent and not a concerted effort.

"Does that help?" Clara asked with a wince.

I leaned over the breakfast table and kissed her forehead. "More than you know."

Thinking about this new information gave me pause. Like other members of the Kings, the idea of ambushing the Angels with murderous intent had crossed my mind. Of course I didn't have it in me to stage a massacre but the thought had been there. Thank goodness we didn't get any further with that plan. Slaughtering innocent people would just earn us the death penalty and a warm spot in hell on the other side.

Chapter 18

Clara

I POURED ZOE ANOTHER glass of wine.

"No," she protested, "enough."

"Have one more," I encouraged her. "I can drive you home."

"I don't want to make you drive me," she worried.

"Then spend the night."

She erupted into giggles at the thought. "It would be like a regular sleepover."

"Alice is probably in bed by now."

"For sure," my best friend agreed. "I put her down myself before I came over here."

"Then just call Patrick and tell him you're too drunk to drive."

"Oh, honey," Zoe put her hand over mine, but picked up the wine glass just the same.

"What does that mean?"

"I can't spend the night." She took a deep sip, giving me mixed messages. "I'll take a rideshare."

I shrugged. "It's up to you. My door is always open."

"Except it isn't," she observed, setting the glass down on the coffee table.

We were seated in my living room, enjoying each other's company. Neither of us had the energy to go out but Zoe had wanted to see me. It had been two days since the barbeque and Jasper's sleepover. I went to work on Monday and Tuesday and it was normal. It was so normal, I felt disconnected from my life.

116

Everyone at the office was talking about the restaurants they ate at and children's birthday parties they had been to. One guy was a rock wall enthusiast and he waxed on about the new climbing gym he had discovered. No one else was involved in a life-or-death struggle between two warring biker gangs. It felt surreal.

Jasper and I had been texting but we hadn't seen each other since he left on Sunday. I didn't feel like he was ghosting me though. He had stuck around to have breakfast and gave me a kiss before leaving. We were in regular contact like a normal couple. I sent him googly eyes before going to bed and he sent me back a heart. When I woke up, I texted him *Good morning,* and he responded by the middle of the day with a complementary message.

Tuesday night, Zoe called and basically invited herself over. The first half hour was just the two of us catching up. I urged her to drink more than her habitual single glass of wine and she appeased me by starting on a second. It didn't escape my notice that she took her time with it. On the other hand, I didn't have to go anywhere so I was free to indulge. I finished off my second glass and poured myself a third.

"So, when are you going to tell me what's going on?" Zoe asked finally.

I licked my lips. The bottle we were working on was a California red. It was sweet, with the taste of grapes and other floral notes. It was one of my favorites and I was happy to have someone to share it with.

"I don't know what you're talking about," I said dramatically.

"Okay." She rearranged herself on the sofa, preparing for a long speech. "When I was here this weekend, Jasper was hiding in the closet."

"Bathroom."

"Whatever." She sighed. "You were going on a date with Simon but for some reason there was some intrigue involved. I saw in the newspaper that Jasper's brother was killed."

"You saw that?" I gulped.

"In the crime section. There wasn't a lot of information but they definitely said homicide and they definitely said Clay Ayers." She fixed me with an expectant stare. "So what's going on?"

I dropped my head back in an exaggerated gesture of frustration. I didn't want to drag Zoe into this. That was the reason I had neglected to hide out at her house several days back. But it seemed like I had no choice. I couldn't put her off any longer and if I stuck to my story and lied to her, I might lose a friend.

"We think that Simon killed Clay," I admitted.

"What?!" Zoe snapped, uncrossing her legs and leaning forward. It was a slap in the face, I understood, and yet the depths of her reaction startled me. That was the theory that Jasper and I were working off of. It seemed rational to me but watching Zoe's face, I wondered if I was crazy.

"He threatened me," I ticked off the reasons we thought Simon was involved. "He's an asshole, and just now when I went to the barbeque with him, he smirked when Davy offered a toast in Clay's memory."

"That's it?" Zoe scoffed. "He smirked?"

"Didn't you hear me?" I demanded. "He threatened me."

"How?"

"He said he knew where I lived and that I had to come with him to Nomad that night or he would hurt me."

"He said that?"

I pressed my lips together and nodded, not trusting myself with words.

"Clara," Zoe tried, reaching out for my hand.

"I remember very clearly that Davy threatened me," I responded.

"Who is Davy?"

"He's the leader of the Angel's Death gang."

Zoe leaned back in her seat, terrified by the story I was telling her. "The Angel's Death? That sounds so horrible."

"Jasper and his friends are the Kings of Hades," I said.

"Yeah but, that's Jasper," she relented, apparently feeling differently about the Kings. "What was he doing hiding in the bathroom?"

"He just wanted to make sure I was safe," I replied.

"While you went off with Simon?"

"Yes."

"And do you really think Simon is capable of murder?"

"I don't know," I answered. "I hope not but I'm really worried that he is. I found something out at the barbeque."

Zoe pressed her lips together, waiting for me to elaborate.

"I don't think Davy knows anything about how Clay and Vince died."

"Who's Vince?" Zoe gasped.

"He was the leader of the Kings before Clay."

"Wait—" She put a finger in the air, struggling to fit all the pieces together.

"He was killed just like Clay," I connected the dots.

"Oh my goodness." She turned pale, her eyes wide and haunted. "Clara, what are you involved in?"

"I'm just trying to do the right thing."

"The right thing is to get the hell out. If they know where you live, move."

"I own this house," I argued. "I can't just sell it."

"Why not?" She seemed panicked, terrified for my welfare even though I didn't have any solid evidence. "You could rent a place. You could stay with me."

"I can't stay with you." I took a gulp of wine before continuing down a path that I didn't want to tread. "I won't put you and Alice in danger like that."

"What about Patrick?" Zoe asked, offended even though I hadn't meant anything by the omission.

"I don't care about Patrick," I teased.

Zoe reached for her wine glass and emptied half of the liquid down her throat. "Have you been to the police?"

"With what?" I demanded. "I don't have any real proof. It's just a feeling. Jasper and the guys know that at least one of the Angels is involved. We thought it was the entire gang, but now we're wondering if it's just Simon."

"I can't believe you used to date the guy," Zoe mumbled.

"Me neither."

"Patrick is going to flip when I tell him."

"You can't tell him," I said quickly.

"Why not?" she complained.

"Because he'll want to go to the police."

"Because that's what people do when they think they're dating a murderer," she said with consternation.

"Not if they don't have proof," I told her.

Zoe looked away, unconvinced.

"The Kings want to handle this on their own," I explained.

"What does that mean?"

"I don't know," I said honestly. I didn't know, though I could guess that there would be some retribution involved. There might be a fight and it might escalate. But that was none of my business and I didn't want to betray Jasper by denying him the right to avenge his brother. As long as we could be sure Simon had acted alone, he deserved whatever he had coming to him.

Zoe picked up the hem of her shirt and worried it between her thumb and forefinger. "I don't like it."

"There's something else," I remembered Jasper's parents from the night before and the secret I had overheard on the porch steps.

"I'm not sure I can take anything more," Zoe said with a weak smile.

"It's not about that," I assured her. "It's about Jasper."

Taking courage from my tone, Zoe leaned forward with interest.

"He invited me to his house for dinner a few nights ago and his parents showed up. Well, it was his mom and his stepfather. Except that when they left, they hung around outside for a moment." I blushed, recounting how I had listened in without them knowing.

"You were spying on them?" Zoe gasped.

"It was... it just happened," I excused myself.

Zoe gave me a look that was at once scolding and encouraging at the same time. It was the look only a true friend could give. She wanted the details as much as I did and was all in to hear them no matter how devious the methodology had been.

"They said that Jasper's stepfather is his real biological father," I finished triumphantly.

"What?" The news had her reaching for the wine glass again. She scrutinized the remaining liquid with a smile. "I'm definitely going to have to get a rideshare."

I ignored that last statement and answered the first question. "I don't know. Jasper's father died a while ago. He was in a car accident. I never met this new guy but if he's really Jasper's father, then who was the man who raised him?"

"Oh shit," Zoe whispered. "What are you going to do?"

"I can't tell him," I said.

"You have to."

"I can't. It's not my secret."

"Maybe you misunderstood."

"Maybe." I chewed my upper lip. "I think I need more information."

"Can you talk to her? To Jasper's mom?"

"What would I say?" I asked, feeling ridiculous. "I'm sort of dating your son, can you tell me intimate details about your family?"

"She knows you," Zoe counseled me, "it's not like you're a stranger."

"Still..."

Zoe shook her head. "Are you sure this is the life you want?"

I laughed. That wasn't the question I was expecting. It wasn't the life I wanted exactly but Jasper was the *man* I wanted. I didn't care if it was in a house in the suburbs or in an apartment in the city, either way, there was only one person for me. The drama between the Kings and the Angels was all consuming. I was more involved than anyone with the exception of Simon and Jasper. Even Davy and the rest of the Angels were in the dark.

I couldn't have walked away if I wanted to. Jasper meant the world to me and I knew Simon was onto our game. I was caught in the cross hairs and I had to see it through. No matter what happened, I would stand by the Kings. It wasn't a choice so much as an obligation. Without realizing it, I had begun to think of myself as a member of the gang.

Chapter 19

Jasper

AFTER ALL THAT HAPPENED between learning of Clay's death and devising the plan to stake out the barbeque, it was hard to believe we hadn't laid Clay to rest yet. I was so totally focused on solving the crime that I didn't pay any attention to the normal bereavement process.

My mother handled most of the arrangements. I shouldn't have let her do it, or at least, I should have helped. I was the oldest child, the only child she had left. I could have been an adult, stepped up and taken charge, but I was busy.

Mom called the funeral home and made arrangements to have the body delivered from the morgue. She picked out the casket, a task that no mother should have to do. She put a notice in the paper and it was a moving tribute to my brother's short life.

Clay Ayers, beloved son, brother, employee, friend, and boyfriend, departed this earth suddenly. He leaves behind his mother, father, and brother, Jasper Ayers. Clay was well known at the bike shop where he worked; his love of motorcycles led him to scour auto auctions in search of bargains to fix up and sell. He will be missed terribly. In lieu of flowers, please make a donation in Clay's name to Toys for Toddlers.

Reading it, I was sure Mom wrote it herself. How she found the strength necessary to sum up her son's life in a single paragraph, I couldn't say. I wouldn't have been able to. Anybody who knew him would understand that didn't even scratch the surface of who he was.

But she couldn't very well put in all the stuff about him keeping a bunch of high-strung bikers out of jail.

I didn't know what was happening with Clay's house either. Presumably we would have to clean it out and put it on the market. I didn't want to have anything to do with that but I knew I couldn't escape it. Making my mother sift through Clay's belongings all by herself would be inexcusable. Hopefully we could let a few months pass before tackling that project. I wanted to ignore it as best I could.

I had to survive the funeral first. I had to comb through all the well-wishers and the sympathizers, all the people who knew Clay and wanted to pay their respects. I felt like a walking corpse. Being with Clara made a big difference but I was a long way from being whole. All I had to do was show up, yet even that seemed monumental.

As soon as Mom told me where and when it would be, I let the rest of the gang know. I contacted Clara and asked if she would like to accompany me.

"Of course," she said.

"You don't have to," I assured her.

"Yes I do," she argued. "Clay was my friend too."

I drove by her house to pick her up. As before, I circled the block to make sure she wasn't being watched. There were no other motorcycles out front and no one stalking the house that I could see. I made a second pass and pulled into the driveway.

Walking up to her front door, I was aware I was on camera. I pushed the doorbell, feeling awkward and out of place. This type of formal event wasn't my speed. The guys and I had an informal ceremony just the night before. We'd gathered in Clay's front yard and poured out a drink for him.

I felt his memory slipping away. It had been little more than a week since I saw him last but already I was thinking of him in the past tense. I felt like the mourning period should have been longer. I wanted to drown my sorrows again and again until there was nothing left. Yet

Clara brought me to my senses, and I was grateful to her. It was because of her that I was sober enough to go to the funeral.

She answered the door wearing a short black dress. I didn't often see her dressed up, and the sight was a welcome diversion. Even though it was specifically for a funeral, I couldn't help but notice how the skirt accentuated her hips. It wasn't revealing or inappropriate in any way but I didn't think it was designed for a grieving outfit. It was more like a cocktail dress.

She had a purse with her. That wasn't a regular occurrence either, since we rode everywhere on a bike. A purse would just get in the way, but I could tell she didn't have any pockets. She locked the house as I waited and together, we walked back to Clay's bike. I didn't kiss her. For some reason, that seemed like it would be in poor taste. We could get reacquainted later, after the service.

I was still riding Clay's bike. I hadn't picked up mine from the impound lot yet and I didn't feel any hurry to do so. There was something about the bike that made me feel more connected to my brother. It was as if I was carrying a piece of him around with me wherever I went. It was comforting and I didn't want to give it up. That, and I didn't want to give the city the satisfaction of paying the release fee. It was probably a couple hundred bucks and I didn't have a lot of extra room in my budget. Clay's bike was doing me all right for the time being and I thought he might have approved.

I settled onto the seat, scootching forward to give Clara room to climb on. She swung her leg over the side, the skirt fitting nicely over her thighs. It was the perfect length for riding. It wasn't so long that it would get caught in the wheels and it wasn't so short that it would reveal anything intimate.

She hugged me tight as I set off, headed for the funeral home. We weren't a religious family so the service wasn't going to be held in a church. Mom had gotten a plot in a city graveyard, one that had a large footprint just outside of town. I suspected that Martin helped her out. I wanted to be thankful that he was there for her in her time of need but I couldn't shake my dislike for the man. No matter how many hoops he jumped through or how many mountains he moved, I would always think of him as a busybody.

We coasted up to the funeral home and found dozens of bikes in the parking lot. I zeroed in on the Kings' motorcycles and parked right beside them. Clara got off and we prepared to make our appearance. She touched her hair, making sure everything was right. Straightening out her dress, she shimmied a little and I couldn't help watching.

"Are you okay?" she asked gently.

"No," I said.

She offered me her hand and I took it. I was done pretending that I didn't care about her. We hadn't made any formal declaration, but I thought it was safe to say that we were officially dating. I wasn't going to be with any other woman and she wasn't interested in another man. We cared about each other and shared a bed occasionally. That was all the proof I needed.

We walked into the venue hand in hand. I was immediately struck by the number of people in attendance. There weren't just bikers and their wives, but friends and customers from work. There were people I had never seen before, older people and people with young children. Maybe they were friends of friends or my mother's inner circle.

It was touching to see how many people cared. It was so easy to get caught up in day-to-day life, not even realizing the value of the people around me. I liked Clay, but he was my brother; I was supposed to like him. All these people were here because they wanted to be. They took time out of their day to come and pay their respects, and that meant a lot.

I made waves instantly as people recognized me. I didn't even know half of them but they all knew me. They came up and put their hands on my shoulders, offered to shake, and gave me their condolences.

I put my game face on to accept the outpouring of support. I didn't realize how well known and well-liked Clay was. As soon it began, I understood why. He was charismatic and responsible. When he said he would do something, he did it. At work, he was friendly and efficient. He fixed people's bikes right the first time and even went the extra mile to upgrade things that he found problematic.

There were friends from high school and friends from trade school. Clay had a degree in small engine repair and there were at least a dozen or so people at the funeral who had studied alongside him.

I thought I would be overwhelmed and that I would hate every minute of it, but seeing how much he meant to other people really struck a chord. Clara was by my side, understanding that I needed the support. She smiled and shook hands with the best of them, assuming her role as my girlfriend naturally.

When I got to the back of the room, I found the Kings MC standing near the casket. Red and Cade were half dressed up in formal attire with suit jackets and ties over jeans. Al and Andrew wore the full funeral uniform with dress pants and everything. They must have made quite a sight on their way to the event.

I was wearing the only formal suit I had, a leftover from my mom's wedding. It wasn't black but charcoal grey, something that I judged was somber enough for the occasion. Together with Clara, we looked more like we were going to a fancy dress party.

Jennifer held onto Red's arm. He didn't seem to mind, playing the leaning post for the afternoon. I gave her a hug, knowing that she was just as grief-stricken as I was. As soon as we parted, Clara went in for an embrace, drawing Clay's girlfriend away from Red for a moment.

The two women held on to each other. Clara seemed to understand that Jennifer needed her more than I did at that moment. She pulled the grieving almost-widow away from the body and sat her down in the front row. They spoke quietly to each other and I couldn't hear them over the murmur of the crowd. It didn't matter. I was sure that Clara was saying something soothing like *Clay is free of worldly concerns now and we just have to be strong.* Whatever it was, Jennifer nodded, her face pale.

I stayed with the boys for a moment before spotting my mom coming toward me. Reluctantly, I left my friends and put my arms around her. She broke down the moment she touched my chest, leaving a deep blue stain on my suit jacket. I followed Clara's lead and walked Mom to a chair. We sat down together and I held her close.

It was bad enough to be at my brother's funeral but to have to provide emotional support was almost beyond my capacity. I was a mess. No one should have to look to me for advice. Yet I did what I could for the woman who had brought me into the world. She was all I had left of Clay. We were alone together, if you didn't count Martin. Our little family just kept getting smaller.

The funeral director called the event to order. In quiet tones, he explained how the process would work. It was simple. There was a guest book everyone was asked to sign that the family – Mom – would be able to take home. The body was on display at the front of the room and if the mourners would get into a line, everyone could pay their last respects.

After an hour of that, the body would be placed in the hearse and the mourners would move to the cemetery. There would be some words spoken by a preacher who worked for the funeral home and afterwards, the body would be interred. Guests were welcome to leave flowers, or they could make a donation to *Toys for Toddlers*. Mom made that determination by herself. Clay had no special affection for the charity but it was one that had deep ties in the biker community. Having been a biker herself once, Mom had fallen back on her knowledge of the community.

I didn't bring any flowers and I wasn't going to make a donation. I had other things on my mind, specifically getting revenge for Clay's death. That was how I would honor him, not through some meaningless gesture or twenty-five dollar gift.

I left Mom with Martin and went up to get in line. I made eye contact with Clara as she sat holding Jenny's hand. She shook her head. Either Jenny wasn't ready to view her boyfriend or she already had. The gang spied me and collected around so that we moved as a group past the rows of chairs. No one gave them any grief for cutting in line. It wasn't a buffet.

As we approached the coffin, a hush fell over the entire club. This was our leader, our brother, mine and theirs. He was the one we were trying to avenge, the person who had done his best to keep us out of trouble. I was determined to honor his memory and at the same time, uphold his name. Just because he didn't want to see us in jail didn't mean we couldn't make Simon pay. We would just have to be strategic about it.

I looked down, expecting to see the same face from the morgue. Whoever did the makeup and the costume had done a good job. He looked almost life-like. Gone was the gaping hole in his face. I squinted to see the stitches running across one cheek, they were hidden so well by concealer. The funeral home must have given him a glass eye because you could hardly tell that there had been any injury.

I would have to remember to thank them for giving Clay dignity in death. I was sure that's what they did day in and day out, but it was appreciated. The rest of the guys hadn't seen what I saw, so they didn't know enough to be impressed. I wondered if I could just reach down into the box and shake him awake.

The ride to the cemetery was a show of strength. There were at least three dozen bikes, most of them clients and friends outside the gang. Mom used to ride back before she settled down and there were still some lingering friendships with old bikers who showed up to pay their respects. Customers from the garage came and while most of them were weekend warriors, some were gang members from across the state.

And of course, the Kings rode side by side, filling the streets with the sounds of our engines. Clara hung on tight. Jennifer rode with Cade, so I guessed she was just hanging on to anyone and anything that reminded her of Clay. I let the sound of so many motors take me away. There was peace in the show of respect. No matter what Simon or Davy might do, they couldn't take this away from me.

We pulled into the parking lot and got off our bikes. Three rows deep, the showing was amazing. I would have taken pictures if I cared. I saw some other people doing that but I couldn't be bothered. There were a lot of things I wanted to remember about Clay, but his funeral wasn't one of them.

We circled the grave site and the finality of the ritual hit me. This was the last time Clay would be above ground. We were planting him in a pit and though we might visit, we couldn't resurrect him. He was finished; it was over. Suddenly I just wanted to be done with it and get the hell out of there.

The preacher was nice, if that kind of thing can be appreciated. I wondered if that's all he did for a living, wander around to random people's gravesites and give blessings. I was all for a dangerous lifestyle but that just seemed morbid. He didn't know Clay and he didn't know our family. Clay had never been to church, not since we were little and Dad made us go for Easter. The thought of a religious ceremony made my stomach flip. I didn't want to disrespect Clay in any way, and having some old guy talk about heaven and hell just seemed wrong.

I kept my mouth shut, though. Interrupting the proceedings wasn't the right thing either. Best just to let the guy speak, do his bit, and then leave. I glanced around at the guys but found them all staring into the grave. We gathered in a circle, the silence deafening.

The coffin slid slowly into the hole, lowered respectfully down into the depths of the Earth. I didn't cry but I saw Mom turn away. Clara squeezed my hand, as if sensing that I needed comfort. I pulled back. It wasn't the time for a show of weakness. I needed to remain strong if I was going to finish the job in front of me.

After it was over, Clara touched my arm. "I'm going to talk to your mom."

"Okay," I muttered.

It made sense that she would want to give her condolences but I was anxious to leave. I couldn't ride away without Clara so that meant I had to stick around. I looked for the gang and found them clustered a few feet away behind someone else's headstone. Remembering the ceremony we held the night before, I wished we had a beverage to pour out. Somehow that seemed more appropriate than standing around in church clothes listening to a preacher.

I looked across at Clara, wondering what she was saying to my mom. The two had never been close. Even back when the family was whole and Clara and I were officially dating, Mom wasn't particularly warm to her. Clara didn't seem to mind. They had a very hands-off approach to each other so I was surprised that their conversation seemed to be taking a while.

I was about to go find out what they were talking about when I heard the sound of more bikes joining the parade. It didn't occur to me to worry at first. Some of the guests were leaving and the sounds of engines sparked the afternoon regularly. But this was different. This was a number of bikes all at once and they were approaching the cemetery, not leaving.

I turned at the same time as Red and Cade. We took a look at the parking lot, disgusted to see the Angels pulling up as one. *The bastards!* I thought, ready to fight. How dare they crash my brother's funeral when they were the ones who put him in the ground? I don't know what they wanted, but I was going to find out one way or another. The Kings were with me as we marched across the field.

A few of the other guests understood what was happening. Anyone connected with the biking scene knew the rivalry between the Kings of

Hades and the Angel's Death. Even those who didn't know what was going on glanced nervously at the new group. There was no mistaking the animosity in the air. One large group of men riding up on another and all of them acting tough, it was enough to scare most of the mourners away.

The people who stayed gave us a wide berth, hovering near the gravesite or deep in the boneyard. They stayed clear of the parking lot, leaving it to us to chase down the intruders.

Chapter 20

Clara

I WALKED AWAY FROM Jasper, determined not to let him see me cry. He was being stoic so I thought it was only fair that I do the same. I hated funerals, although to be honest, I didn't have a lot of experience with them. It was Jasper who had buried his father, or the man he thought was his father. It was so confusing.

I knew that it wasn't the right time to confront his mother but I couldn't think of when such a conversation would be appropriate. Everyone was offering words of kindness, and I got in line. When it was my turn, I gave the woman a hug. She had been crying but seemed calm for the moment.

"I'm so sorry," I said, unsure how to begin.

"Thank you," she replied. "It's wonderful to see you and Jasper back together."

"We're not—" I started but then stopped myself. If she was actually happy to see us reunited as a couple, I didn't want to deny her that small pleasure.

Seven years ago, when Jasper and I first went out, I didn't exactly get along with his mom. She was a retired biker babe who had found happiness in her home with her husband and family. I knew she was still a bit of a drinker and she pulled out a cigarette as I watched. She lit it up without asking if it was okay.

We were alone for the moment and I knew I wasn't going to find a better time. I sealed the deal with a breath and plunged ahead. "I wanted to talk to you about something."

She raised her eyebrows, allowing me to continue.

"The other day when you were over at Jasper's house—"

"Sorry about that," she said, puffing on her smoke. "I know you overheard some shouting. It's hard for Jasper."

"It's hard for you too," I observed, "but that's not what I meant."

"Go on."

"Jasper went down into the basement after you left and I...wanted to see you safely to your car." There was no good way to admit that I'd been eavesdropping but I wanted to paint myself in a good light. "I overheard your husband say that he was Jasper's real father."

The woman gasped, almost dropping her cigarette. She looked around wildly, checking to see if anyone else had heard. There was no one within earshot and she relaxed a modicum, knowing her secret was still safe.

"You can't tell him that," she whispered.

"I won't," I promised. "I haven't. But is it true?"

She looked pained. I understood that it was a painful subject and a burden that she didn't want to carry. I could only imagine what kind of twisted web had resulted in such a development. It was none of my business and I felt intrusive, yet my desire to know outweighed my caution.

"Yes, it's true," she admitted. "I will tell him. I just don't know how."

"I'm sure he just needs time to get to know..." I paused, grasping for the man's name.

"Martin," she supplied.

"Martin," I repeated. "Jasper's dealing with a lot right now. He's not himself."

The woman scoffed, resuming her smoke. "He is most definitely himself. He didn't like Martin from the beginning. Now that Clay is gone..."

I felt sorry for the entire family. There I was, picking at old wounds during a funeral. It was unkind and I struggled for a way out of the conversation. "He'll come around."

"And if he doesn't?"

"He will," I said. "I'm sure of it."

Jasper's mom regarded me critically. "Maybe you know him better than I do."

I snapped my jaw shut. The last thing I wanted to do was get into some kind of pissing contest with her. She was Jasper's mother, and that meant a lot. He might be a grown man but he was still her baby. I only knew him as an adult and half that time we were separated. I let the matter drop, scanning the graveyard for a distraction. What I found was not exactly what I had in mind but it definitely took the spotlight off our little argument.

The parking lot was set at the edge of the lot. There was a wrought iron fence that surrounded the yard, cutting it off from the cars. But a massive gate was flung open for the mourners, creating yards of open space for people to move back and forth.

The Angel's Death gang were standing on the opposite side of the fence, looking in. A few of them were still on their bikes but some had already parked. I could identify Davy and Dom, that bastard who choked me behind Nomad during the bar fight. I didn't see Simon immediately but that didn't mean he wasn't there.

A chill raced up my spine. It was a cold act of defiance for them to show up at the funeral of a man they had killed. Yet my rational brain was still working. I reasoned that Davy thought he was being kind. His words at the barbeque came back to me, seemingly honest and respectful. Maybe he didn't understand what was really going on. Maybe this was his way of burying the hatchet.

I scanned the funeral crowd, looking for Jasper. It wasn't hard to find him; he was plowing through the onlookers on a direct collision course to the party crashers. I started to follow him. This wasn't the time or the place for a gang fight. He misunderstood what was going on, I was sure of it.

Davy didn't mean to provoke the King's anger. He was trying to do the right thing. It was Simon who was the murderer and the only one who didn't belong. It was as if I could see the entire encounter unfold before it even began. Clay's funeral would devolve into a fistfight and all the regular guests would run screaming to the edge of the graveyard.

I hurried to catch up to Jasper, to stop him before he did something stupid. Clay's spirit might demand retribution, but not at his own funeral. Surrounded by family and friends, it should be a dignified affair.

I had all the words ready but someone stopped me before I could reach him. I looked over to see Jennifer. She pulled me back, forcing me to turn away. I saw the rest of the Kings streaming after Jasper, a show of force that could not be misunderstood.

"I have to stop them," I protested.

"If Simon sees you, it will just make things worse," Jennifer said.

"But they're going to ruin Clay's funeral," I argued.

"There's nothing we can do," Jennifer responded wisely. "You can't get between them. It'll never work. And if the Angels see you after what you did, there'll be hell to pay."

I sighed in anguish. As painful as it was, I knew Jennifer was right. How was I going to stop five hotheaded guys from defending their turf? Any gesture I made would be futile, and if the Angels got wind of me, I would be condemning myself to who knew what. I followed Jennifer's lead to the back of the crowd, blending in with the regular folks.

We paused at a safe distance and turned back to watch.

Chapter 21

Jasper

I WAS SO ANGRY; I COULDN'T see straight. How dare they crash Clay's funeral? Those bastards were going to pay. I plowed through the funeral crowd, feeling but not seeing the rest of the Kings collect behind me.

We were five strong, not nearly as impressive as we once were. Vince was there too, in spirit. His body lay beneath the ground a few meters from Clay's. There wasn't another municipal graveyard within twenty miles. I felt the energy of our two fallen members bolstering our ranks. They might have crossed over, but their loyalty could never be questioned.

There were more Angels physically present. That simple fact was enough to make my blood boil. We might be bastards but we weren't murderers. They were the ones with that market cornered.

"What the hell are you doing here?" I demanded, striding through the gate.

Some of the lesser Angels looked concerned, as well they should. What did they think was going to happen? That we would welcome them into our circle of grief? That we would plant a seed of friendship over the fallen body of my blood brother? I wondered what had gone down at whatever meeting they called to order before arriving on the scene. How had Davy convinced them it was a good idea?

Look guys, we killed two Kings but let's show up to pay our respects. Was that what Davy had said? And the rest of the Angels had simply gone along with it? The audacity was too blatant to wrap my head around. I was going to make sure they regretted that decision, no matter what the cost.

"We just wanted to offer condolences," Davy said.

"Bullshit," I snarled. "You're here to gloat."

"Do you think I had anything to do with this?" Davy demanded.

"Damn right I do," I continued forward, getting up into the man's face.

"We draw the line at murder," the leader of the Angels said.

"You're the lowest scum on the planet and a fucking idiot if you think I'll buy that," I roared, hauling back to strike him in the jaw.

Red grabbed my arm, pulling me back at the last minute. I struggled, desperate to sink my fist into Davy's ugly face. Red was like an octopus; every time I tore myself loose, he had another arm ready to restrain me.

"You want to fight?" Simon stepped around his boss, his eyes burning with the same fury that overtook me.

I hadn't seen him before; he blended in so well with the rest of those hoodlums. If Davy was misguided, Simon knew exactly what was going on. Even without proof, I was sure that he was the author of my brother's demise. I switched gears, itching to put Simon in the ground along with the fallen Kings.

Red still wouldn't let me go. I pulled up abruptly, stepping back and straightening my jacket. My friends saw that I had calmed down and they released me. It took all my energy not to launch back into the attack.

"I definitely want a fight," I said as soon as I composed myself.

If it was me against Simon with no interruptions, I was sure I could win. He was a low-down, slimy little monster, and as long as he didn't have a gun, I knew victory would be mine. It would be a delight to pound on his face, to beat him into the ground and kick him when he was down. I might even kill him with my bare hands, I was that livid. My confidence was so great, I didn't even bother to consider the facts.

Clay had been shot. He was beaten and then fired upon, not bested in a fair fight. Of course Simon would come armed. He knew he couldn't beat me man-to-man. I would have to be prepared for anything he might throw at me but in that moment, I didn't care. All I wanted to do was tear into him. That urge was paramount, supplanting all but the most basic instincts. I was sure I could take him.

"Let's go," Simon said.

I noticed that his friends weren't holding him back. Either they didn't care or they were too caught up in their own bravado to worry about fighting at my brother's funeral. I felt Red tense beside me and heard Cade crack his knuckles.

"Not here," I said. "I'm going to bury my brother first, then I'm going to put you in the ground."

"Big words," Simon sneered.

"Your funeral's next," I promised.

"Where and when?"

"Next Tuesday at Our Lady of Garbage," I spat.

"The fight," Simon corrected me. "When and where are we going to fight?"

"The parking lot of the old Kroger," I named a desolate spot just outside of town.

The old Kroger hadn't been in business for years and the parking lot was in disrepair. It was a known hang out for high school kids after hours and played host to the occasional squatter. It was the perfect place to kill someone in private.

"I'll be there," Simon said.

"We'll all be there," Davy threatened.

"One hour," I said.

I stood back as most of the Angels got back on their bikes. Davy stuck around reluctantly. I was beginning to get the feeling that underneath all the macho bullshit, he really did care. It was too bad, because it didn't matter. He was the leader of the death squad. He had chosen that role, and no amount of peacemaking was going to change that.

The Angels had been formed in retaliation for the death of Davy's brother. Davy blamed the tragedy on Vince and did everything in his power to strike back. Maybe Simon had killed Clay, but that didn't make Davy innocent. If he really wanted to make peace, he could tell his boys to back off. But he didn't do that. Instead, he was going to show up on the opposite side and watch me duke it out with Simon.

My affinity toward Davy didn't extend very far. Just because he might not be aware of everything that happened under his nose didn't make me feel all warm and fuzzy. He was the leader. If Simon was going rogue and killing people without permission, that didn't speak well of the gang leader.

Maybe he didn't know that one of his soldiers had killed Clay. Maybe he thought he was being friendly by riding up on us like this. But he was missing a few screws if he thought that would matter. I was going into the fight with both eyes open. We were going to take down as many Angels as possible, starting with the worst one.

Davy had made his bed. I wasn't going to pretend to be moved by his show of respect. He was the reason Clay was dead. Even if he didn't pull the trigger himself, he set the wheels in motion. I turned away before he could say anything more. He didn't deserve my time.

"I'm sorry for your loss," Davy called out, mounting his bike.

I gave him the finger as I walked away. Returning to the warm embrace of my friends and family, I geared myself up for the fight. There were just a few things left to do. I had to say goodbye to my mom and her husband. I had to put in one last appearance before I would be able to ride off.

Clara and Jennifer met us as we approached the grave site. The coffin had just been lowered in and people were still clustered around, throwing flowers down into the hole. They looked up, uncertain if the drama in the parking lot had concluded. A few of them were just waiting for their chance to ride off, not at all interested in witnessing a gang fight. They said one last prayer over Clay's coffin and then hurried away. I watched them go like rats abandoning ship.

I didn't see Mom. The last place I had spotted her was behind a tree, having a cigarette and talking to Clara. When I looked back at that spot, it was empty. I would have to find her to let her know I was leaving.

"Hey," Clara said, catching my attention.

"Hey," I responded, distracted.

"What do you mean hey?" she demanded.

"What do you mean?" I parroted. I was quickly getting confused. Was she angry with me and if so, why? I was completely focused on paying my last respects so that I could get out of there and meet up with the Angels.

"What's going on?" Clara said, doing a little head bob to catch my attention.

I looked down at her, not sure whether to be amused or annoyed. "I'm going to meet with them."

"Why?"

"To fight, of course."

"Where? When?" She adjusted the purse strap against her shoulder and I was reminded that we were all in our Sunday best. Fighting in these clothes wouldn't be ideal, but I didn't care enough to drive home and change. I would just have to trash this suit and buy a new one for Simon's funeral. If he thought I was going to stay away from his event after he crashed Clay's, he was mistaken. I was going to bury him six feet deep and then play the part of a mourner, devastated by the loss. After that, I would spit on his grave.

"The old Kroger," I replied. "In an hour."

"Fifty minutes," Red corrected me.

"I'm coming with you," Clara said.

I shook my head. "You should go home. I'm sure my mom will give you a ride."

"I don't want to go home," she answered stubbornly, planting herself in my path.

I was still looking around for Mom, eager to get that one chore out of the way before breaking skulls. Clara was fierce, as determined as I had ever seen her. But she was crazy. After the barbeque, the Angels would have it out for her. She had barely escaped. I knew, because she told me that Simon was on to her before she left. If I hadn't been there to pick her up, who knows what might have happened.

I might be eager to get involved but I wasn't ready to put Clara in any danger. She would be better off at home and I wasn't going to be the one to take her there. I would just have to ditch her. She could get a ride with my mom or she could take a rideshare. The logistics didn't matter; what mattered was that she got home safely and that she stayed far away from the parking lot where the fight was going to go down.

"I don't have time to argue with you," I said.

"Then don't," she replied. "I'm coming with you."

"Clara," I tried, heaving a great sigh. I looked around to my friends for help but found them all engrossed in other activities. Red was looking at the sky and Cade was studying the ground. They were trying not to get involved at the very moment that I needed backup. "What if Simon sees you?"

"Let him," she snapped. "I don't care. I want you in my life. I want all of you, the good and the bad."

That got my attention. I reached for her hand, taking it firmly in my own. We stood several feet from Clay's grave, staring lovingly into each other's eyes. What had I done to deserve her devotion? Nothing, to my knowledge. She had more fire than I had any right to expect and I was tempted to let her stay.

"What about you?" Cade asked Jennifer.

"I'm going home," she said. "I don't want anything to do with this."

"We're fighting for Clay," Red reminded her.

"You're fighting for yourself. Clay didn't want anyone to die," Jennifer replied, sticking her chin out in defiance.

"That was before he was murdered," Andrew grumbled.

Jennifer narrowed her eyes and I could see we weren't going to convince her. She was the perfect match for Clay, all soft curves and pragmatism. She was right about one thing; if Clay was alive, he would have tried to rein us in. He was forever advocating for peace and rational thought and some of us, like Cade, considered that to be his undoing.

It was past time for negotiations. The Angels threw that olive branch away when they showed up here. I wanted to punish Simon for everything he had done, not only to Clay but also to Clara. Jennifer was sweet but she wasn't going to talk any sense into me. I appreciated her willingness to step aside rather than argue.

I still had to find my mother, and that was the priority. I decided to consider Clara's ultimatum. If she wanted to come with me, would I really do her any service by denying her request? Maybe we were destined to be together like that. Maybe Simon wasn't powerful enough to keep us apart.

"Okay," I mumbled. "I have to tell my mom that I'm going."

"She's over there, with your... with Martin," Clara said, pointing at the guard house.

I picked up Clara's hand and together we walked across the green to say goodbye. The sun was shining and the birds were chirping. There were a few trees in the graveyard and they were remarkably full of life. I was reminded that they were probably sucking nutrients out of the dead people. It made the picture a whole lot less pretty when I thought about it that way.

Mom and Martin were arguing about something quietly. They ceased as soon as Clara and I walked up. Mom flashed a smile. It was good to see her coherent enough to engage in pleasantries. I wasn't going to spoil her day by letting her know where I was going.

"Clara and I are going to take off," I said.

"Stay," Mom prompted, reaching out for Martin's hand. "There's a reception after."

"I can't." I leaned forward to kiss her on the cheek. "I'll see you later."

"I'll hold you to that," she said, putting a hand on my shoulder.

I gently extracted myself from the embrace. It just wasn't the time. I needed to focus and get my head in the game or I was going to lose the battle before it began. My mom would have to soldier on by herself. We were both mourning the same person, but from opposite ends of the room. I felt bad, but not bad enough to stay.

Chapter 22

Clara

IT DIDN'T TAKE JASPER long to find his mother. He said goodbye without making any reference to the fight that was about to happen. I stayed with him throughout, holding onto his hand. It was partly to shore him up but partly to satisfy my need for human contact. I felt dizzy and lightheaded, as if I would float away without an anchor.

His mom looked at me, worried that I might have spilled her secret. I shook my head gently to let her know that I was sticking to my part of the bargain. She seemed relieved, though if she knew what Jasper was up to, she would be horrified. I tried to pretend that everything was okay. We were just going back to my place to watch some television or the whole gang was going to Wheelie's to enjoy sandwiches and pie. Whatever we were doing, it definitely wasn't meeting Simon's gang behind a decrepit grocery store for a potentially lethal fight.

Jasper's mom kissed him on the cheek and opened her arms to me for a hug. I obliged, feeling overwhelmed. So much was happening, I didn't know where to start. As we walked away, Jasper pulled me in close.

"She likes you," he said.

"I don't know about that," I objected. "I think we just came to an understanding."

"No," he countered. "She likes you. I can tell."

"Well, that's a good thing, isn't it?"

"A very good thing," he said with a grin.

I was caught off guard by the simple gesture; it was so out of place at a funeral. We weren't supposed to joke or smile. It was a solemn occasion and the appropriate reaction was one of pain and sorrow. Jasper's smile was like the sun, warm and life giving. I wanted to hold it fast, to make it last forever. But just as quickly as it appeared, it was gone.

We walked through the gate to the parking lot along with the rest of the Kings. Getting on our bikes, we peeled away from the cemetery together. I knew I would have to face Simon. There would be no more hiding. He knew what I had done and he knew that I was no Angel. I was a King through and through. I might not own my own bike but I was committed to the cause just the same as the rest of the guys. If Jasper went down, I would go down too. We were two halves of the same whole and I was ready to share his fate.

It was a ten-minute ride to the Kroger, on the outskirts of town in the opposite direction as the cemetery. I braced myself for a violent display. I was no virgin to gang fighting; in recent days I had witnessed two brawls, one at Nomad and one at Wheelie's. I knew this one was going to trump them all.

There would be no bartender to call the police, no innocent customers to run screaming for the hills. There would be no authority figures to break it up and with only the two gangs in attendance, the likelihood that the violence would result in death was very real indeed.

I told myself that I could handle it. If Jasper was there, I wanted to be there too. I needed to see his triumph or failure with my own eyes just in case he didn't come home. I wanted to be there until the very end, and if necessary, keep his secrets.

We pulled into the grocery store parking lot and found the Angels waiting for us. We parked a few meters away from them, probably so they couldn't mess with our bikes. Dismounting, the Kings straightened their jackets.

We had straight from the funeral and everyone was wearing their best attire. It was a little incongruous, a bunch of bad-ass biker dudes about to have a fight dressed in suits and ties. I followed Jasper as he approached the rival gang.

There was dissention in the Angel's ranks. Davy and Simon started arguing just as we approached. The rest of the Angels stood around, looking menacing while the two of them had heated words.

"It's not right!" Davy shouted. "You can't kill a man on the same day as his brother's funeral."

"It's not your problem!" Simon shot back.

"I'm the leader of this gang, I'm making it my problem," Davy snarled.

"Piss off. The Kings are ready to fight. I can't take that away from them," Simon argued with an evil smile.

Davy growled, turning his back to the other man in disgust. I could see that he wanted to apologize to Jasper but he wouldn't. There were lines he couldn't cross even in sympathy. Any show of weakness would be devastating for his position as leader of the gang. Even though he empathized with the Kings for the loss of one of their own, he couldn't go so far as to say anything comforting.

I shook my head. It was almost more pathetic that he wanted to be kind but wouldn't. My own experience with Davy was mixed. He obviously wasn't an angel even though that was the name of the gang he rode with. Before the fight at Nomad, he had said something truly awful to me and yet seeing his pragmatic side I wondered if it had been all talk. Maybe he didn't mean anything by the threat and was just blowing hot air.

Simon was leading the gang. I couldn't see it any other way. Davy might have the title but Simon was the real power behind the throne. He did what he wanted and he got away with everything. If he killed Clay, he did so without official orders. Davy's days as gang leader were numbered; I could see that clearly. He was losing what little control he had to Simon's insidious cancer within the group.

I didn't like Davy but I liked him more than Simon. He seemed to want to turn a page, maybe soften the conflict between the two gangs. If that was the case, he was worse than naive. Both Simon and Jasper were ready to kill. If either of them had their way, the other would be leaving the parking lot in a body bag.

"Kill him!" Theo said wickedly.

"Turn him into a piece of meat," Dom encouraged.

Simon cracked his knuckles, staring daggers at Jasper. For his part, Jasper was a lot more circumspect. He walked to one side, gathering all the Kings into a pre-war conference. I hung back, letting them talk. Whatever details they needed to iron out didn't involve me. They put their heads together, whispering so that none of the rest of us could hear.

I found myself alone, pushed out of the group and standing apart from the Kings. I felt out of place in my little black dress. It was perfect for a funeral or for a night on the town, but less so for a violent altercation. I was overdressed just like the rest of them, but for some reason they wore it well and I felt like an idiot.

There were no other women in the parking lot. All the wives and girlfriends had stayed home. I was the only one brave enough or stupid enough to follow my man to the hunting grounds. Simon walked over, sizing me up with a lurid glance.

"I knew you were working with the Kings."

I looked to Jasper for help but he was deep in conversation with the rest of the guys. He didn't even notice that his sworn enemy was approaching me. I straightened my spine, determined not to give him the pleasure of seeing me afraid. I would show him. He couldn't make me back down any more than he could make Jasper walk away. The two of us were inseparable and Simon was about to come face to face with that reality.

"I'm not sorry I lied to you," I said. It sounded childish but that was how I felt. Lying was wrong in most circumstances but when you needed to know if someone killed your friend, it was more than acceptable.

"You're a good liar," he replied, circling me like a vulture.

"So are you."

"I never lied to you," he snapped.

"What about when you said you gave a shit?" I spat.

"I don't recall ever saying that I cared about you," he purred, so evil it was despicable.

I laughed. It was almost amusing, hearing his take on our story. I wasn't in love with him by any means, but there was a time when I thought we had a connection. Apparently he never had a kind thought in his heart for me. I was always just a means to an end. It would make watching his downfall a lot easier.

"There was a time I thought we were friends," I said. "But that's over. You're disgusting."

"And you'll spread your legs for any biker," he retorted, pleased with himself.

"You're going down," I promised him. "And I'm here to witness it."

"The winner of the fight will get to take you home." He winked, imagining that he would be the victor. "And you won't like what I'm going to do to you when that happens."

"I'm with Jasper," I said, forcing my stomach to remain in its place. Just the thought of going home with him again made me sick. Whatever happened, whether Jasper won or lost, I was never going to go back to Simon. That chapter of my life was over, thank goodness. I didn't care if he had to kill me, I would never submit to his advances again.

"You're with me, baby," Simon replied, licking his upper lip.

I stuck my finger down my throat, a juvenile gesture but one that had the desired effect. Simon scowled, lunging toward me in contempt. Jasper might have been distracted but he saw that movement. Before Simon could reach me, my hero broke free from his peer group. In an instant, Jasper was between me and the threat, reaching out to grasp Simon by the lapel.

Simon wasn't ready for him and it took a moment for him to register the large biker in his path. He came up short, lowering his arm and transferring his attention from me to my boyfriend. Jasper didn't give him the time to reconsider, hitting him full force in the nose with a closed fist.

Simon staggered back, cupping one palm to his face. Bright red blood began to drip from between his fingers. I backed up instinctively, rushing over to where Red, Cade, and the others were standing. The time for talk had passed. The fight had begun.

Chapter 23

Jasper

———◆———

I JUST WANTED TO MAKE sure that my guys were clear on the parameters of the fight. I was the one who was going to take Simon down. Not Cade, not Red, and certainly not Andrew; they would all have to wait their turn. If the thing spilled over into a gang-on-gang skirmish then they would have their chance to get dirty. Until then, I wanted them to hold their ground.

I had just reiterated my desires when I heard Simon and Clara talking behind me. Turning to face them, I saw him step toward her. I cursed myself again for leaving her in the line of fire. If it wasn't for blind luck, Simon would have had ample opportunity to abuse her at the barbeque and possibly at her own home.

I was struck with an overwhelming need to protect her. It wasn't about Clay anymore, and it certainly wasn't about me. The honor of the Kings faded into the background and for the moment, the only thing that mattered was Clara's safety.

I had allowed her to come with me against my better judgement. She was stubborn and I could see that she wasn't going to take no for an answer. She had been with us at Nomad when the shit hit the fan, so I knew she could handle herself in a fight. I didn't have to remind myself that I had rescued her there too. I was crazy if I thought she could just wander around in the land of the Angel's Death without an escort. She had a bright red target painted on her back and it was all my doing.

Without a second's hesitation, I stepped between the two of them, raising my fist and grabbing Simon's jacket. I plowed into him, not giv-

151

ing him time to bring his hands up in self-defense. I felt the satisfying crunch of cartilage breaking and I knew I had done some damage.

Behind me, Clara moved to the side, giving me space to take up the fight. Simon staggered back, released from my death grip and putting his hand to his nose. Blood leaked through closed fingers, indicating that I had done my job. He was wounded already and it didn't bode well for him.

His beady little eyes narrowed and he dropped his hand from his face, curling his fingers into fists. He came on suddenly, like an arrow released from the bow. I danced to the side, easily avoiding him and launching him out into the wilderness of the parking lot.

He recovered, his face grim. He lunged at me again. This time I held up my fist, connecting with his shoulder as he tried to break through my defenses. He stomped on my foot and sent his elbow rocketing toward my temple at the same time.

I pulled my leg back, shaking the outraged appendage. I leaned away from his swing, narrowly missing the connection. Simon was fast but I was faster. I knew I didn't look it, but I had a lot of skill when it came to fighting.

It's an interesting thing. There's not a lot of respect in the general public for people who can hold their own in a fight. Having been in my fair share, I can say that the activity is ninety percent mental and only ten percent physical.

You have to keep moving. I never let my feet stop. No matter what was going on, I was constantly shifting, looking for an opening, watching my opponent for signs of an attack. If he came at me from the left, I moved to the right and struck out as he passed. If he came at me from the right, I went left. If he shifted his weight, that was an indication that he was preparing another blow. All of these things ran through my mind with terminal velocity, creating a whirlwind of strategy that I had to get ahead of.

I cleared my thoughts. There was only room for one thing at the moment, and that was the fight. I had to forget about Clara and Clay, forget about my feelings of abandonment and love. I forgot all about my mom and her idiot husband. I had to focus on what I was doing or risk getting stomped.

Simon was good. After recovering from my first, second, and third blows, he came back with a wicked kick to the thigh. He seemed to be going after my legs. I kept that in mind as I circled. My foot still hurt from where he had stomped on it. I didn't think anything was broken, because I could still walk, but the pain was creeping into my consciousness and distracting me from my task.

He aimed for my knee next, cutting into it with the tip of his boot. I chopped down with my right hand, catching a punch before it could land. All around us, the Kings and the Angels cheered. Each time I struck home, all my friends would scream encouragements and each time Simon got to me, the Angels sent up a war whoop.

We danced back and forth across the pavement. Simon got through my blockade and knocked me to my knees. I rolled away and came back before he could finish the job. My palms were scraped and my leg ached. He kept pushing that same limb, each kick aimed for the same spot. It was infuriating but also helpful. At least I knew where to look for his next assault.

I ran into him, fed up with the slow pace of the struggle. He grabbed my shoulders as he fell, pulling me down on top of him. We rolled around on the ground, the hard surface of the road slamming through me. I felt the fabric of my jacket rip just as I knew it would. It wasn't meant for this kind of abuse.

I got the upper hand, punching him twice before he twisted away. He scrambled to his feet, kicking me once in the rib cage before I came back up. I was tired and there were a thousand points of contact all over my body that ached. He was breathing hard, sweat pouring down his face to mix with the blood on his upper lip.

I swung again, missing him as he bobbed. He struck me in the side again in exactly the same spot as he had kicked a moment before. I felt a stab of pain and the breath flicked from my lips, leaving me empty and vulnerable.

I reached down to grab him by the wrist, pulling him close before he could get away. He struggled in my grasp, knowing that he had made a mistake. I came around the side of his head with my elbow, digging into his ear and his eye socket at the same time.

A cry escaped him, something between a gasp and a curse. He fell to the ground, his entire body going limp. I doubled over in pain, taking a moment to catch my breath. The surface of the parking lot swayed beneath my feet. I planted my palms against my knees, pressing my eyes closed.

Beneath me, Simon stirred weakly. He brought one knee up and the released it to the ground again. I fell down beside him, grabbing his shirt and punching him in the jaw. He didn't have any fight left in him. I knew in that moment that his life was mine if I wanted to take it.

Around us, the Kings and the Angels started to stir. A few of Simon's comrades moved toward me as if they were going to push me away from their friend. Some of the Kings stepped up to block them, determined to let me have my vengeance.

I kicked Simon in the chest, too angry to fight fair. He groaned and rolled into a ball, the only thing he had the energy left to do. I stumbled back, out of air myself. I might have won the fight but winning had taken its toll. I was sore from head to toe and so tired I was seeing spots.

On either side of the divide, a champion for rationality stood up. Red moved in front of the Kings line and Davy stopped the Angels from advancing.

"It was a fair fight," Red said to dissuade the Kings from attacking.

"Let him fight his own battles," Davy cautioned his men.

I spat in Simon's general direction, though I missed connecting with him and hit the ground. Staggering away, I found Clara by my side. She tucked herself neatly underneath my arm, shouldering some of my weight.

I smiled down at her, pleased with myself. I hadn't killed the man but I had given him plenty to think about. I was sure that was the last time he would mess with the Kings. Even his stupid head had to grasp the implications of our fight. Every breath he took from here on out, he owed to me. I was the one who had chosen not to kill him, to give him the gift of life for as long as he could hold onto it. With his track record, I was sure someone else would finish the job. It was only a matter of time.

I was heading toward my ride, determined to get away from the scene when Simon inched his way up off the pavement. Not only was he not dead but he was still conscious. I didn't care. The lesson had been taught, as far as I was concerned.

"Enjoy your victory while it lasts, King," the man choked out, enraged that he had allowed himself to fall so far.

I didn't pay any attention. Swinging my leg over one side of the bike, I waited for Clara to get on behind me. Once we were both astride, I raised the kickstand and took off. I was riding high off Simon's defeat. I knew that I could beat him when it came right down to it, and I wasn't disappointed.

I didn't really want to kill him. There was a lot of anger and a lot of talk but I wasn't a murderer. I didn't want to go down for the rest of my life over a piece of scum like Simon. There were too many witnesses. I might trust the Kings not to say anything but the Angels were another story. The first thing they would say if they got nabbed for a petty offense was *I know who killed Simon Mortimer.* Not only that, but I just didn't have it in me.

A beating was one thing but when it went too far, more lives would be ruined than just the victim's. I didn't know if Simon had family but he certainly had friends. Escalating the gang war was the last thing that

Clay would have wanted. And Clara... what would she think if she saw me kill a man?

I realized that I had left Simon with the option to come back at us again but for the time being, we were safe. And if I kicked him a few times when he was down it was just to serve as a reminder of my power. So long as he came at me honestly, I could beat him. I could protect Clara and dish out vengeance for both Clay and Vince.

Behind us, I heard the spark of half a dozen engines and I knew that the parking lot scene was breaking up. We had avoided an all-out war and proved once and for all that the Kings were dominant. After burying Clay, I felt some measure of satisfaction. Simon had been punished for showing up at the funeral. It might take a few more beatings before I was convinced to leave him alone. If he had been involved in Clay's murder he deserved at least that. But for the time being, everything was right again. I would cross the next bridge when I came to it.

I drove to my house without thinking. Dropping Clara off at home alone didn't seem like an option. She had just walked through hell and back for me, twice. I wasn't going to let her go. I pulled up the driveway and parked beneath the awning. Locking the bike up took almost more dexterity than I had at the moment.

Clara had to crouch down to retrieve the chain for me. I thanked her with a weak smile. Even though I was the victor, Simon had gotten in a fair number of punches. I could feel sore spots on my face, hands, chest, and legs. Everywhere I turned, another body part protested. It was going to be a long few days of recovery, that was sure. But it was worth it.

Before Clay was killed, I hardly ever locked my bike up. But now that I was riding around on my brother's motorcycle, I took extra precautions. I wouldn't put it past the Angels to regroup and try something dirty like messing with a guy's bike after a fight.

I looped the chain through the front wheel and around the chassis before locking it tight. Clara popped up and inserted herself underneath my arm. I didn't really need the help, but I accepted it. She was just taking care of me and I thought it was sweet. I needed to get inside and investigate all the bruises. I was willing to let a lot of things slide, but I wanted to know the extent of the damage.

We walked awkwardly to the front steps where Clara stood back to let me open the door. Inside, there was nowhere to sit except the couch. Clara helped me over and I slid down onto the seat gratefully. Sometimes the couch was hot and uncomfortable but sometimes it was warm and welcoming. This was a welcoming time; I didn't think I had ever been so glad to be home.

Clara locked the door behind herself, dropping her purse beside the door. She came around and knelt in front of me, reaching for one of my shoes. I watched her work, in awe of every movement. She was so kind and gentle, almost like a deer who had wandered into my house. I wondered how I could be so lucky. It wasn't every guy who had such a loyal girlfriend. I hadn't asked her to come with me but she had showed up anyway and saw it through to the end.

She took one foot and lay it on her knee, unlacing my boot inch by inch. It was almost erotic the way she paid close attention to her work, easing my foot free. She set the boot down on the floor beside the couch and reached for the other one.

The act was so tender and loving, I almost forgot that Clay was gone. The day had been consumed with the funeral and the angst of the fight afterwards. But now it seemed that things had turned around. I wasn't a grieving family member anymore, I was a king in every sense of the word.

When she was done with my shoes, Clara moved on to my socks. I felt a tiny prick of embarrassment. She was so close to my feet and they were unwashed. I wondered if I could coax her into the shower again but the weight of exhaustion crowded in on me and I put my head back.

I felt her fingertips stroke the bridge of one foot. There was a tiny bit of pain, causing me to open my eyes again. I looked down to see an ugly red spot just below my calf. I remembered the fight and how Simon had stomped on me there.

I wanted to move my foot out of her lap but she held it firm. After a long moment, she rose and sat down beside me. Like a nurse, she continued to undress me. Sliding one hand beneath my suit jacket, she slid it off my shoulders. I rose up off the back of the couch to help, pulling one arm out and then the other.

Every time I moved, I winced. I was a walking bag of bones, a meat sack that had taken a beating. She pulled the jacket into her lap to examine it. There were a few holes and streaks of dirt on the elbows and in the back. I wouldn't be wearing that article of clothing again.

Without a word, she draped the jacket over the empty couch cushion, treating it as gently as if it were a thousand-dollar suit. I just watched her, mesmerized by her dedication. She leaned forward and began to undo my tie.

I threaded a finger through the knot, releasing it from around my neck. It was a wonder Simon hadn't used that against me. I could just imagine choking on the modicum of respectability I had managed to pull off.

She slid the thing free and lay it lovingly beside the jacket. I was starting to get turned on. I wondered if I would have the strength or the energy to make love to her and decided I would rally. It would be the perfect end to a day of sadness. Clara was my rock; she was my heart and soul and I wanted nothing more than to bury myself deep inside her.

She returned to her task, unbuttoning my collar. With careful deliberation, she unfasted one clasp after another until my shirt hung open down to my waist. I felt her hands gliding down my chest, coming to rest at a particularly painful spot.

Following her gaze, I saw a strawberry red mark consuming my lower rib cage. I had been kicked there more than once. Her fingertips grazed over the unbroken skin, her touch light as a feather. I felt myself sinking into pleasure, her attention erasing the bruises.

We removed my shirt, leaving me naked from the waist up. I wanted to kiss her but I didn't want to break the spell. She eased me forward so she could take a look at my back. I followed her lead, gazing at her with a questioning eye as she shook her head.

"No blood," she reported.

"That's good," I said with a smile.

She reached a hand up to stroke my beard. We were heading for the same place, just taking our time getting there. I put my hand against hers, pressing her palm to my face. She smiled at me but I could see the tears hovering just beneath the surface.

"I'm sorry," I whispered.

"For what?"

"For dragging you into this."

"You didn't drag me into anything," she said stubbornly. "I'm the one who started to date Simon. I did that all on my own."

I released her hand. "Don't remind me."

"You beat him good," she said.

I nodded but even that movement was painful. It felt like my brain was sloshing around in my head and I had to close my eyes to regain my balance. Her fingertips touched my eyebrow, tracing the curve of the hair across my forehead. As if by magic, the headache was gone.

I reached up again, this time using more force. I took her hand in mine and pulled her close. She didn't resist, meeting me halfway with a kiss that was hot and passionate. It was as if I had unlocked a door and let a monsoon of desire run free.

She repositioned herself, coming closer, pushing up against my thigh. I knew there were more injuries we hadn't discovered yet, but this detailed examination of my body was turning me on. I could look at myself in the mirror after I had my fill of Clara. Whatever it might take, no matter how much it hurt, I was determined to have her.

I helped her up into my lap and then gasped as the sudden transfer of weight sent pain blasting through my core. She hopped off, breaking the kiss and widening her eyes in horror. I exhaled, feeling relief after the burden was gone. Clara put her hands on her hips, acting more like a scolding wife than a sexy lover.

"Take your pants off," she said.

"Yes ma'am," I replied with a grin.

I stood up, bracing myself against the couch. She watched me move, her gaze calculating. I could see she wanted me as much as I wanted her but that she wasn't interested in doing anything that would cause me pain. I sighed, digging deep for the strength I needed.

My cock was already growing hard, aroused to action by her loving touch. I wasn't thinking straight. The only thing that mattered to me was showing Clara I was fit for duty. I undid my fly and pushed the suit pants down to my knees.

Wincing, I realized I would have to move around to take them completely off. She sat on the edge of the couch, not offering assistance. It was as if she was judging my competency, and I wanted to impress. I set my jaw, stubbornly pushing the pants all the way to the floor. My junior soldier pushed out against my underwear, telling her everything she needed to know about my state of mind.

Clara focused on the tent for a moment, her eyes lighting up. Then she tore her gaze away, scanning my legs for signs of abuse. One knee was battered. It wasn't black and blue yet but it was a deep shade of red. I knew I was in for a painful few days with that one.

Clara reached out to touch my knee, skimming her fingers lightly over the skin. I'd had enough. I'd showed her that I was man enough to fuck her; now it was time to collect my payment. I reached down, scooping her up into my arms.

She gasped, shocked that I still had the strength for such a maneuver. I crossed the room and mounted the steps. My bad knee almost gave way under the added weight but I pushed through. Tossing Clara up over my shoulder, I allowed myself to use the banister. Holding her in place with one hand I climbed up one step at a time. It felt like it took forever but it was really only a minute.

At the top, I set her down.

"You shouldn't—" she began.

"Get in the bedroom," I commanded.

She snapped her jaw shut, seeing the determination in my eyes. She didn't argue, racing away across the hall. I gave myself one final moment of rest before diving in. I could sleep when I was finished. I needed this, for my body, my mind, and my soul.

Chapter 24

Clara

AS SOON AS JASPER ORDERED me into the bedroom, I understood. He was walking with difficulty but he wasn't seriously injured. Or, he might be seriously injured but he didn't require a doctor's care. He was healthy enough to be horny and that was good enough for me.

Examining his body, I could see all the places that were about to turn purple. I wondered what Simon looked like, if Jasper wore so many scars. Simon had gotten in a few punches and a few kicks but Jasper had wiped the floor with his enemy. It was a good bet that Simon would need some stitches or at the very least, a splint.

I grinned. I didn't want to admit it even to myself but the fight turned me on. It was so powerful watching Jasper defend my honor. When Simon said that about me going home with the victor, I didn't have a doubt in my mind that it would be Jasper. Even if Jasper didn't win, there was no way I would have followed Simon to his bed. He would have to kill me first.

But when Jasper rained that first punch down on the Reaper's head, I cheered inside. When Jasper continued to land punches and finally thrashed the fiend to the ground, my inner slut did a happy dance.

I couldn't wait to take Jasper home and lick his wounds for him. I didn't care who knew it; I was proud to be sleeping with my man. What made things even better was that Jasper had stopped himself before killing his opponent. If there had been a murder, everything would have changed. We would have a secret to keep and I would be a witness to a crime. As it was, I could relax knowing that we had won.

I just wanted to make sure that Jasper was okay before jumping him. I was careful to touch him gently, to remove his clothing piece by piece so that I wouldn't miss anything. My eagerness must have been obvious because he caught on pretty quickly.

When he walked me up the stairs, I held on tight, praying that he would be okay. He wouldn't be the first guy who injured himself trying to impress a woman. I hoped Jasper knew what he was doing.

He made it to the top and prompted me to go to bed. I hesitated briefly, hoping I was making the right choice. I didn't want to hurt him anymore than he was already hurt, but it seemed that he was up for the job.

Darting into the bedroom, I left the door open. What he was doing in the hallway, I didn't know. I didn't care either. I figured I had less than a minute before he would join me and I wanted to set the stage.

I pulled the covers down on the bed, pushing them away to create a smooth surface for our activities. I unzipped my dress, struggling to reach the clasp at the back. Peeling the garment off, I laid it on a chair. I stepped out of my shoes and my bra and my underwear, getting naked without any further ado.

Jasper arrived just as I was laying my undergarments on top of the dress. I whirled, inhaling deeply. He stood before me, dressed only in his boxers. He was a beautiful sight, pure masculinity, a warrior who had won my heart.

I tugged at my ponytail, releasing the locks to cascade down my back. I knew how much Jasper liked to play with my hair while we screwed. Shaking it out, I smiled seductively at him. I crossed the room, colliding with him halfway between the door and the bed.

He didn't bother to shut the door. We were alone in the house with no chance of intrusion. I combed my fingers through his hair, bringing his lips down to mine. He reached around me, planting a hand on my ass. We were about to become one, and it felt insanely good.

My breasts squished against his chest; my rib cage pressed to his rib cage. The solid wall of his body flexed as he inhaled and relaxed as he exhaled, a piston engine right when I needed one.

I dropped my hands from his head and ran my fingers across his shoulders. They were so broad, I felt like I could keep going all day. When I reached the end, I smoothed down his biceps, remembering how powerful they were when they were pounding into Simon.

I wanted Jasper, possibly more than ever before. I knew I was crazy, that it wasn't right to be so turned on by a fight. But the heart wants what it wants. I moved from his biceps to his back, not caring what anyone thought of me.

His spine curved inward, then my hand found his buttocks. I pushed past the barrier of his boxers, inching them down across his ripe flesh. He helped me out, breaking contact for a moment to discard the last remaining obstacle.

Then we were free, both naked and standing right next to the bed. I sat down on the mattress and he followed me, as hungry as I was. I pushed him back, having something else in mind.

His cock was rock hard between us, standing at attention, toying with me. I licked my lips, ready to consume him. Going down on my knees on the hardwood floor, I slid both palms up his legs. From this vantage point, I could see the growing bruises and I knew they were bad.

Ignoring it all, I took hold of him by the base. With one hand, I cupped his balls, and with the other, stroked his manhood. He took me by the hair, winding his fist through my locks. I was trapped but happy to provide this service. Opening my mouth wide, I took the plunge.

The tip of his cock slid across my tongue, filling the void in my chest. I inhaled and pressed forward, swallowing him whole. There was no pause for foreplay or for tantalizing licks of the masthead. I went from zero to sixty in less than a second, gorging myself on his rod.

He groaned, leaning back ever so slightly to give me a better angle. I relished the taste of him, the feel and the size of his member. He deserved this after such a strenuous battle. I was the wicked temptress, the maiden that he had won. He was my champion and the only man I wanted.

I sucked hard, sliding my lips across his flesh. He struggled to remain still as long as he could but when the pressure became too much, he began to help me out. Rocking his hips back and forth, he thrust deep.

I gagged on the intrusion, loving every minute of it. He was so strong and forceful, a warrior through and through. I lavished him with affection as only a lover could do. Swallowing him again and again, I felt myself growing wet.

He stopped right as it was getting good, pulling me to my feet by my hair. Without worrying about where my mouth had been, he kissed me. Pushing me down onto the bed, he leaned over. I saw him wince as he climbed on top of me and knew that he was in pain. Selfishly, I ignored it. He was a grown man; he could do what he wanted. The heat of the moment came first and everything else was just noise.

I spread my legs for him, welcoming him in. He took a second to look down at me and smooth the hair from my face. I lay open to him, ready for his conquest. He took his dick in one hand and guided it to my opening.

The pressure was intense as he slid his way inside. I moaned, my eyes fluttering open and then shut, unable to decide which was best. I stretched my chest out, my nipples erect and greedy for his attention. He lowered his torso so that we met in the middle and I could feel the plated muscle that lay beneath his skin.

He gave me only moments to adjust, my tunnel stretching to accommodate him. When he began to move, I saw stars dancing before my eyes. This was what I wanted. This was what I needed. My entire body had craved his affection from the moment Simon went down until Jasper penetrated me with his weapon.

I latched onto his shoulders, holding fast as he rode me. Bending my knees, I allowed him to go even deeper. He pierced my soul. I cried out, desperate for release. The pressure built, dragging me toward a monumental conclusion.

He paused for a moment to lean back, lording above me while we were connected. He reached for my legs, draping them across his shoulders. When he resumed his thrusts, I was bent into an untenable position. I couldn't help him; I could only lie there and take it.

He beat down upon my intimate zone without mercy, taking us both away. My orgasm came first, reaching up out of my core to drench my body with its light. Dimly, I felt Jasper thunder on, bracing himself to empty his load. He dug deep, grunting with satisfaction when he reached the high-water mark.

Waves of relief washed through me, spreading out from my stomach to my toes. We had done it. We conquered the mountain. We beat back the Angles and arrived in paradise together, shining and brand new.

Jasper let my legs drop and collapsed on top of me. His breath came hot in my ear, proof that I had exhausted him just as he exhausted me. I put a hand on his back but he only stayed there a moment. Rolling off, he slipped out of me. Grunting with pain, he lay beside me, shoulder to shoulder.

After a long moment, I rolled onto my side, propping my head up on my elbow. "Do you want to take a shower?"

"No," he grumbled. "But I probably should."

"I'll be gentle," I teased.

He glanced at me, his angular face awash with humor. We got up and walked to the bathroom, holding hands. He reached into the shower to turn on the water, glancing at himself in the mirror. I ogled his butt while he did it, satisfied but always in the mood for another round.

I wanted to go at his speed though, which meant making sure that he was comfortable. Being able to look at his entire body, I could see multiple abrasions and red marks. Simon really worked him over.

Jasper caught me looking and pulled me into his arms. "I'm okay."

"I'm glad you beat him but I wish you hadn't let him land so many punches," I said.

"Hey," he protested, giving me a kiss. "I did my best."

When the water was warm, he pulled the shower door back, gesturing to me that I should step inside. I put my hand under the stream and found it warm. Getting in, I made room for my playmate. He filled up half the shower stall, relegating me to the far corner.

I found the bodywash and poured a dollop on my hand. Lathering up, I began to wash him. He gazed at me in contentment as I soaped up one arm and then the other. Running my hands along his shoulders, I stroked his neck. Dropping down to his chest, I rubbed his pectoral muscles and then his abs.

He grabbed the bodywash from its place near the wall and squirted some into his hands. Taking his time, Jasper did the same for me, washing all the dirt and grime from my skin. If we hadn't already expended our energy, we might have worked ourselves up to another climax. As it was, he was fighting to remain upright.

I could see that I wasn't going to get anywhere and so I let him wash his own privates. He couldn't reach his legs without a large amount of pain, so I crouched and did them for him. There were a few scrapes and dozens of bruises but no open wounds. Though I wished he didn't have any injuries, I could see that he wasn't in bad shape. It could have been worse.

We finished our shower and stepped out, each reaching for a towel. There were two on the rack; one was big, the other was small. I had to use the small one and it barely fit around my chest. Jasper didn't say anything, though his eyes sparkled with the joke.

Going back across the hall to the bedroom, he gave me some sweats to wear. I didn't have anything except the black funeral dress and I wasn't anxious to put that back on. Jasper's pants were eight sizes too big and I had to knot the drawstring to keep them up. His T-shirt smelled like him and it was wonderful.

I was finally comfy and warm, satisfied and tired. We laid down in bed together, having no energy for anything else. Jasper wrapped one arm around me from behind. I pressed my spine into his chest and we spooned, drifting off after a long, hard day.

"I love you, Clara," he murmured.

I gasped. I couldn't help it. The words were electric, magic even. I heard a sharp intake of breath from behind me and realized he hadn't meant to let them slip out. His body tightened and I rubbed against him to let him know I appreciated it.

The depth of his feelings took me by surprise. Without Clay, I knew I was the closest person in the world to him. He still had his mother, but they were estranged. The guys in the gang were close friends, brothers even, but no one he wanted to spend the rest of his life with. It was eye opening to hear him confess his true emotions. I desperately wanted to say *I love you too,* but the words caught in my throat.

I was hiding a secret from him so massive that it would change everything in the blink of an eye. Could I really obey his mother's wishes and keep the information to myself? Didn't Jasper deserve to know?

He had given me his heart and I felt like I was betraying him by not speaking. If I truly loved him, I would share my ill-gotten gains. His own mother was lying to him and had been lying since the day he was born. It had to stop. Jasper had to know.

I cleared my throat, rotating to face him. Within the confines of his arms, I finally spoke. "I have something to tell you," I said.

Chapter 25

Jasper

THE WORDS WERE OUT before I could stop them. I had just been thinking about how much Clara meant to me. Having her to come home to was the best gift a guy could ask for. Having beaten Simon into the ground and avenged Clay's death, I had planted my flag and made sure everyone knew that Clara was with me.

There would be no more subterfuge. She wouldn't pretend to be interested in Simon anymore. I wouldn't let her go anywhere near him. The time for lies and playacting was through. Clara was my girl and I wanted her to know it.

But as soon as I said *I love you*, she stiffened. I knew I had said too much. I was perilously close to sleep and I wasn't thinking of the consequences. I wanted to walk it back, but how could I do that? Once that thought has been uttered, there's no second chance. I couldn't pretend that it wasn't true. Maybe I hadn't given it full consideration but, in that moment and for a thousand moments to come, I knew we were meant to be together.

She rolled over, turning to face me. I thought she might kiss me or say something else to make the admission less awkward but instead, she wanted to talk. I pressed my eyes shut. I was exhausted but suddenly wide awake. I cursed myself for opening the door. What I needed was a good night's rest, not a heart to heart.

I might be good with my fists and I definitely knew my way around the bedroom, but I was abysmal with emotional revelation. I didn't want to have a conversation. I wanted to go to sleep. It was my own fault. I should have stopped the words before they exited my mouth. It didn't make them any less true; it just wasn't the right time.

I groaned, sitting up in bed. I was in it now and there was no way out but through. "It's okay if you don't love me," I muttered, feeling stupid.

"It's not that," she sat up beside me. "I'm glad you told me. I feel the same way."

"You do?" My heart melted. Hearing her confirmation put my mind at ease. "What is it then?"

"I know something," she hesitated. I could see the conflict in her eyes. It must have been something serious because the way she looked could only be called conflicted. "I overheard something," she clarified. "And then I talked to your mother and she confirmed it."

My breath grew cold in my lungs. What information could my mother possibly have shared with Clara that would cause her such distress? Was it something about Clay? Something about me? Something about her and her health? Was my mother sick?

"She asked me not to tell you and I thought that was best because it's really her choice whether to share with you or not," Clara rushed on.

"What is it?" I demanded.

"I felt just awful keeping this from you but it's not my place to tell you and it's really none of my business."

"Clara," I warned her.

"I just don't know what to do. Either way, I'm going to make someone unhappy. But you have a right to know. She should have told you a long time ago."

"What is it?!" I shouted.

She grasped at the covers, pulling them up to her chin. In the light from the streetlamps outside, she looked like a little kid. I was the one who had frightened her but I couldn't worry about that at the moment. I needed to know what she knew. Somehow, it seemed vital.

"Martin is your real father," Clara whispered.

I stared at her for a long moment, not breathing. Had I heard her right? It couldn't be. She must have meant that Martin was my stepfather, which was something that I already knew. Yet as I searched her face in the dim blue light, I saw that she wasn't kidding. It was real. The man I detested, the one that I was constantly rude to and who annoyed me with his parental gestures was actually my flesh and blood biological father.

I grappled with the implications. My mother had lied to me my entire life. All along, I had thought that her first husband was my father. The man who raised me, who taught me how to ride a bike, who taught me how to fix an engine and how to fight, he wasn't my dad at all. Was he even her first husband? How had it worked? Had she gotten pregnant by Martin and then married my father? Was she that much of a lying cheat?

The more I thought about it, the angrier I became. My blood began to boil, sending steam rising up through my veins. What did that mean about Clay? Was he even my brother? Was he my half-brother? Was the man I knew as Dad actually a father to either of us?

When exactly did Martin come into the picture? Had my mother been cheating on my father with her new husband? I came up with a thousand dirty scenarios and I hated every last one of them.

And Clara knew. She had known for days, probably since that night my mother and my stepfather... Martin had come over. She said she cared about me, but that must have been a lie. You don't care about someone and keep something like this from them. She had actually spoken to my mom and together the two women decided to maintain their alliance.

If my mom was to blame, then Clara was equally guilty. I couldn't believe I was spooning with her half a minute ago. I told her that I loved her and it had been true at the time. But with the weight of a few words, all that was in the past.

I stood up, ignoring the protest of my aching legs and sides. I couldn't believe everyone in my life had betrayed me this way. I needed to get out. I needed to ride. There was only one thing that would sooth my anguish and that was getting steel between my legs and watching the road spin out beneath my tires.

I'd had it up to here with women. They were all cowards. I was through with the Angels and with my family. The only people who hadn't done me wrong were the Kings. Clara got up to follow me downstairs, crying and begging for forgiveness. I didn't listen.

"I'm going out," I said, sitting down on the couch to lace up my boots.

"Please, Jasper." She got down on her knees in front of me. I didn't even look at her.

"I want you gone when I get back," I said.

"How?" she gasped.

"Get a rideshare," I growled. "I don't care. Just don't be here."

I grabbed my leather jacket, pulling it on. I was wearing sweatpants but I didn't care. There was nothing fashion could do for me at that point. I needed to clear my head and if it looked like I had run out of the house in my pajamas, so be it.

I stormed out the front door, slamming it behind me. A moment later, Clara followed me out. She was barefoot, wearing my clothes. I didn't care if she took them with her, at the moment I didn't care about anything except my injured pride.

Everyone I thought was on my side had been lying to me. Even Martin, who I didn't appreciate but foolishly thought gave a damn about me, was full of it. I didn't need any of them. I didn't trust them anymore and I didn't want to be around them. I would cut all ties. I felt dead inside. It was as if my entire life had taken a wrong turn and I stood by the side of the road, watching it drive away.

I needed the Kings and I needed a drink, in that order.

"Jasper, wait," Clara said, holding out her arms.

I ignored her, unlocking my bike. She could burn in hell for all I cared; I was that angry. She didn't want to let me go, coming around to grab at my jacket. I pulled away, yanking the leather from her grasp, making her stumble.

She was crying. Tears stained her cheeks and filled her voice as she called my name. "Jasper, please."

I threw my leg over the hog and drove away, leaving her alone the same way she had abandoned me when she made a pact with my mother. I didn't feel like I was throwing her to the wolves. She was the one who had made the biggest mistake. I was the victim; at least that's how it felt.

I leaned on the throttle, trying to put distance between myself and my feelings. It didn't work and yet I needed it to. The implications of the knowledge I had just uncovered chilled me to the core. I was angrier than I had ever been.

The only thing that mattered was the motorcycle club. The Kings were the brothers I never had, my chosen family, my ride or die. I burned rubber all the way to Red's place, determined to forget myself. For a moment, I considered my mother's betrayal. It turned out I didn't know who I was. I knew one thing, though; I was a biker and I was a member of a gang. It was their loyalty that I could trust when everything else was stripped away.

I had no other choice but to turn to the people I understood. I killed the thing inside me that ached for Clara. I didn't need it. She was dead to me, my mother too. All I had left was myself and my friends, and I was about to get drunk to celebrate.

THE END

KINGS
ENTICING
SINNER
LEXY TIMMS
ENTICING
SINNER
LEXY TIMMS
GET IT ON
Google Play
kobo
Available at
amazon
nook
Lexy
Timms

King of Hades MC Series

B ook 1 – Sinner
Book 2 – Tempting Sinner
Book 3 – Enticing Sinner

Find Lexy Timms:

LEXY TIMMS NEWSLETTER:
http://www.lexytimms/newsletter
Lexy Timms Facebook Page:
https://www.facebook.com/LexyTimms
Lexy Timms Website:
http://www.lexytimms.com

Want

FREE READS?

Sign up for Lexy Timms' newsletter
And she'll send you updates on new releases,
ARC copies of books and a whole lotta fun!

Sign up for news and updates!
http://www.lexytimms/newsletter

More by Lexy Timms:

FROM BEST SELLING AUTHOR, Lexy Timms, comes a billionaire romance that'll make you swoon and fall in love all over again.

Jamie Connors has given up on men. Despite being smart, pretty, and just slightly overweight, she's a magnet for the kind of guys that don't stay around.

Her sister's wedding is at the foreground of the family's attention. Jamie would be fine with it if her sister wasn't pressuring her to lose weight so she'll fit in the maid of honor dress, her mother would get off her case and her ex-boyfriend wasn't about to become her brother-in-law.

Determined to step out on her own, she accepts a PA position from billionaire Alex Reid. The job includes an apartment on his property and gets her out of living in her parent's basement.

Jamie must balance her life and somehow figure out how to manage her billionaire boss, without falling in love with him.

** The Boss is book 1 in the Managing the Bosses series. All your questions won't be answered in the first book. It may end on a cliff hanger.

For mature audiences only. There are adult situations, but this is a love story, NOT erotica.

Book 1 – Payment for Sin
Book 2 – Atonement Within
Book 3 – Declaration of Love

A Bump in the Road Series

Book 1 – Expecting Love
Book 2 – Selfless Act
Book 3 – Doctors Orders

Faking It Description:

HE GROANED. THIS WAS torture. Being trapped in a room with a beautiful woman was just about every man's fantasy, but he had to remember that this was just pretend.

Allyson Smith has crushed on her boss for years, but never dared to make a move. When she finds herself without a date to her brother's upcoming wedding, Allyson tells her family one innocent white lie: that she's been dating her boss. Unfortunately, her boss discovers her lie, and insists on posing as her boyfriend to escort her to the wedding.

Playboy billionaire Dane Prescott always has a new heiress on his arm, but he can't get his assistant Allyson out of his head. He's fought his attraction to her, until he gets caught up in her scheme of a fake relationship.

One passionate weekend with the boss has Allyson Smith questioning everything she believes in. Falling for a wealthy playboy like Dane is against the rules, but if she's just faking it what's the harm?

SOMETIMES THE HEART needs a different kind of saving... find out if Charity Thompson will find a way of saving forever in this hospital setting Best-Selling Romance by Lexy Timms

Charity Thompson wants to save the world, one hospital at a time. Instead of finishing med school to become a doctor, she chooses a different path and raises money for hospitals – new wings, equipment, whatever they need. Except there is one hospital she would be happy to never set foot in again—her fathers. So of course, he hires her to create a gala for his sixty-fifth birthday. Charity can't say no. Now she is working in the one place she doesn't want to be. Except she's attracted to Dr. Elijah Bennet, the handsome playboy chief.

Will she ever prove to her father that's she's more than a med school dropout? Or will her attraction to Elijah keep her from repairing the one thing she desperately wants to fix?

THE ONE YOU CAN'T FORGET

Emily Rose Dougherty is a good Catholic girl from mythical Walkerville, CT. She had somehow managed to get herself into a heap trouble with the law, all because an ex-boyfriend has decided to make things difficult.

Luke "Spade" Wade owns a Motorcycle repair shop and is the Road Captain for Hades' Spawn MC. He's shocked when he reads in the paper that his old high school flame has been arrested. She's always been the one he couldn't forget.

Will destiny let them find each other again? Or what happens in the past, best left for the history books?

** *This is book 1 of the Hades' Spawn MC Series. All your questions may not be answered in the first book.*

Don't miss out!

Visit the website below and you can sign up to receive emails whenever Lexy Timms publishes a new book. There's no charge and no obligation.

https://books2read.com/r/B-A-NNL-FOQXB

BOOKS 2 READ

Connecting independent readers to independent writers.

Did you love *Tempting Sinner*? Then you should read *Building Billions - Part 1*[1] by Lexy Timms!

By USA Today Bestselling Author, Lexy Timms.

One night love affair

It was only supposed to be one night. Ashley's just a low step on the ladder of her company's success. The company party was always a big to-do. Jimmy Sheldon, the CEO and found of Big Steps always made sure his employees had a good time. He should, he worked them hard, expected more than they thought they could give, but he always rewarded their efforts. It's what made him a great boss and the owner of a million-dollar company. He knew how to make things work.

And boy, did he.

---

1. https://books2read.com/u/mVZy02

2. https://books2read.com/u/mVZy02

A few too many cosmo's and Ashley hit the dance floor. She forgot how much fun it was to dance. After a few songs, her years of competitive dance routines came back to her and she had everyone trying to move like her. Even boss-man Jimmy. And he had some decent dance moves himself.

From the dance floor to the hotel room, Ashley swore they'd both forget what happened in the morning and go back to their steps on the ladder.

Except, no one ever forgets a hit song...

Building Billions:

Part 1

Part 2

Part 3

Read more at www.lexytimms.com.

Also by Lexy Timms

12 Days of Christmas
Snowflake Hollow - Part 1
Snowflake Hollow - Part 2
Snowflake Hollow - Part 3
Snowflake Hollow - Part 4
Snowflake Hollow - Part 5
Snowflake Hollow - Part 6
Snowflake Hollow - Part 7
Snowflake Hollow - Part 8
Snowflake Hollow - Part 9
Snowflake Hollow - Part 10
Snowflake Hollow - Part 11
Snowflake Hollow - Part 12
Snowflake Hollow - Complete Series

A Bad Boy Bullied Romance
I Hate You
I Hate You A Little Bit
I Hate You A Little Bit More

A Bump in the Road Series
Expecting Love
Selfless Act
Doctor's Orders

A Burning Love Series
Spark of Passion
Flame of Desire
Blaze of Ecstasy

A Chance at Forever Series
Forever Perfect
Forever Desired
Forever Together

A Dark Casino Romance Series
High Roller
Place Your Bet
All Or Nothing

A Dark Mafia Romance Series
Taken By The Mob Boss
Truce With The Mob Boss
Taking Over the Mob Boss

Trouble For The Mob Boss
Tailored By The Mob Boss
Tricking the Mob Boss

A Dating App Series
I've Been Matched
You've Been Matched
We've Been Matched

A "Kind of" Billionaire
Taking a Risk
Safety in Numbers
Pretend You're Mine

A Maybe Series
Maybe I Should
Maybe I Shouldn't
Maybe I Did

A Royal Affair Series
Royally F*cked
Royally Screwed
Royally Obsessed

Assisting the Boss Series

Billion Reasons
Duke of Delegation
Late Night Meetings
Delegating Love
Suitors and Admirers

BBW Romance Series
Capturing Her Beauty
Pursuing Her Dreams
Tracing Her Curves

Beating the Biker Series
Making Her His
Making the Break
Making of Them

Betrayal at the Bay Series
Devil's Bay
Devil's Deceit
Devil's Duplicity

Billionaire Banker Series
Banking on Him
Price of Passion
Investing in Love
Knowing Your Worth

Treasured Forever
Banking on Christmas
Billionaire Banker Box Set Books #1-3

Billionaire CEO Brothers
Tempting the Player
Late Night Boardroom
Reviewing the Perfomance
Result of Passion
Directing the Next Move
Touching the Assets

Billionaire Hitman Series
The Hit
The Job
The Run

Billionaire Holiday Romance Series
Driving Home for Christmas
The Valentine Getaway
Cruising Love
Billionaire Holiday Romance Box Set

Billionaire in Disguise Series
Facade
Illusion

Charade

Billionaire Secrets Series
The Secret
Freedom
Courage
Trust
Impulse
Billionaire Secrets Box Set Books #1-3

Blind Sight Series
See Me
Fix Me
Eyes On Me

Branded Series
Money or Nothing
What People Say
Give and Take

Building Billions
Building Billions - Part 1
Building Billions - Part 2
Building Billions - Part 3

Butler & Heiress Series
To Serve
For Duty
No Chore
All Wrapped Up

Change of Heart Series
The Heart Needs
The Heart Wants
The Heart Knows

Club Confession Series
Envy
Crave

Cottage by the Sea Series
Surging Tide
Distant Shores
Twisting Ocean

Counting the Billions
Counting the Days
Counting On You
Counting the Kisses

Cry Wolf Reverse Harem Series
Beautiful & Wild
Misunderstood
Never Tamed

Darkest Night Series
Savage
Vicious
Brutal
Sinful
Fierce

Diamond in the Rough Anthology
Billionaire Rock
Billionaire Rock - part 2

Dirty Little Taboo Series
Flirting Touch
Denying Pleasure
Forbidding Desire
Craving Passion

Dominating PA Series
Her Personal Assistant - Part 1

Her Personal Assistant - Part 2
Her Personal Assistant Box Set

Fake Billionaire Series
Faking It
Temporary CEO
Caught in the Act
Never Tell A Lie
Fake Christmas
Fake Billionaire Box Set #1-3

Firehouse Romance Series
Caught in Flames
Burning With Desire
Craving the Heat
Firehouse Romance Complete Collection

Forging Billions Series
Dirty Money
Petty Cash
Payment Required

For His Pleasure
Elizabeth
Georgia
Madison

Fortune Riders MC Series
Billionaire Biker
Billionaire Ransom
Billionaire Misery
Fortune Riders Box Set - Books #1-3

Fragile Series
Fragile Touch
Fragile Kiss
Fragile Love

Great Temptation Series
The Devil's Footsteps
Heaven's Command
Mortals Surrender

Hades' Spawn Motorcycle Club
One You Can't Forget
One That Got Away
One That Came Back
One You Never Leave
One Christmas Night
Hades' Spawn MC Complete Series

Hard Rocked Series
Rhyme
Harmony
Lyrics

Heart of Stone Series
The Protector
The Guardian
The Warrior

Heart of the Battle Series
Celtic Viking
Celtic Rune
Celtic Mann
Heart of the Battle Series Box Set

Heistdom Series
Master Thief
Goldmine
Diamond Heist
Smile For Me
Your Move
Green With Envy
Saving Money

Highlander Wolf Series
Pack Run
Pack Land
Pack Rules

Hollyweird Fae Series
Inception of Gold
Disruption of Magic
Guardians of Twilight

How To Love A Spy
The Secret
The Secret Life
The Secret Wife

Just About Series
About Love
About Truth
About Forever
Just About Box Set Books #1-3

Justice Series
Seeking Justice
Finding Justice

Chasing Justice
Pursuing Justice
Justice - Complete Series

Karma Series
Walk Away
Make Him Pay
Perfect Revenge

King of Hades MC Series
Sinner
Tempting Sinner

Kissed by Billions
Kissed by Passion
Kissed by Desire
Kissed by Love

Leaning Towards Trouble
Trouble
Discord
Tenacity

Love on the Sea Series
Ships Ahoy

Rough Sea
High Tide

Lovers in London Series
Risking Millions
Venture Capital
Worth the Expense
The Price of Luxury
Exclusive Passion
Sparkling Christmas
Lovers in London - 3 Book Box Set

Love You Series
Love Life
Need Love
My Love

Managing the Billionaire
Never Enough
Worth the Cost
Secret Admirers
Chasing Affection
Pressing Romance
Timeless Memories
Managing the Billionaire Box Set Books #1-3

Managing the Bosses Series
The Boss
The Boss Too
Who's the Boss Now
Love the Boss
I Do the Boss
Wife to the Boss
Employed by the Boss
Brother to the Boss
Senior Advisor to the Boss
Forever the Boss
Christmas With the Boss
Billionaire in Control
Billionaire Makes Millions
Billionaire at Work
Precious Little Thing
Priceless Love
Valentine Love
The Cost of Freedom
Trick or Treat
The Night Before Christmas
Gift for the Boss - Novella 3.5
Managing the Bosses Box Set #1-3
Managing the Bosses Novellas

Mislead by the Bad Boy Series
Deceived
Provoked
Betrayed

Model Mayhem Series
Shameless
Modesty
Imperfection

Moment in Time
Highlander's Bride
Victorian Bride
Modern Day Bride
A Royal Bride
Forever the Bride

Mountain Millionaire Series
Close to the Ridge
Crossing the Bluff
Climbing the Mount

My Best Friend's Sister
Hometown Calling
A Perfect Moment
Thrown in Together

My Darker Side Series
Darkest Hour

Time to Stop
Against the Light

Neverending Dream Series
Neverending Dream - Part 1
Neverending Dream - Part 2
Neverending Dream - Part 3
Neverending Dream - Part 4
Neverending Dream - Part 5
Neverending Dream Box Set Books #1-3

Outside the Octagon
Submit
Fight
Knockout

Protecting Diana Series
Her Bodyguard
Her Defender
Her Champion
Her Protector
Her Forever
Protecting Diana Box Set Books #1-3

Protecting Layla Series
His Mission

His Objective

His Devotion

Racing Hearts Series

Rush

Pace

Fast

Regency Romance Series

The Duchess Scandal - Part 1

The Duchess Scandal - Part 2

Reverse Harem Series

Primals

Archaic

Unitary

Roommate Wanted Series

The Roommate

The Bunkmate

The Flatmate

R&S Rich and Single Series

Alex Reid

Parker

Sebastian
Zane

Saving Forever
Saving Forever - Part 1
Saving Forever - Part 2
Saving Forever - Part 3
Saving Forever - Part 4
Saving Forever - Part 5
Saving Forever - Part 6
Saving Forever Part 7
Saving Forever - Part 8
Saving Forever Boxset Books #1-3

Secrets & Lies Series
Strange Secrets
Evading Secrets
Inspiring Secrets
Lies and Secrets
Mastering Secrets
Alluring Secrets
Secrets & Lies Box Set Books #1-3

Shifting Desires Series
Jungle Heat
Jungle Fever
Jungle Blaze

Sin Series
Payment for Sin
Atonement Within
Declaration of Love

Southern Romance Series
Little Love Affair
Siege of the Heart
Freedom Forever
Soldier's Fortune

Spanked Series
Passion
Playmate
Pleasure

Spelling Love Series
The Author
The Book Boyfriend
The Words of Love

Strength & Style
Suits You, Sir
Tailor Made

Perfect Gentleman

Taboo Wedding Series
He Loves Me Not
With This Ring
Happily Ever After

Tattooist Series
Confession of a Tattooist
Surrender of a Tattooist
Heart of a Tattooist
Hopes & Dreams of a Tattooist

Tennessee Romance
Whisky Lullaby
Whisky Melody
Whisky Harmony

The Bad Boy Alpha Club
Battle Lines - Part 1
Battle Lines

The Brush Of Love Series
Every Night
Every Day

Every Time
Every Way
Every Touch
The Brush of Love Series Box Set Books #1-3

The City of Mayhem Series
True Mayhem
Relentless Chaos
Broken Disorder

The Debt
The Debt: Part 1 - Damn Horse
The Debt: Complete Collection

The Fire Inside Series
Dare Me
Defy Me
Burn Me

The Gentleman's Club Series
Gambler
Player
Wager

The Golden Game

On The Pitch
Respect the Game
All Game
Sweat and Tears
The Final Score
The Golden Game Box Set Books #1-3

The Golden Mail
Hot Off the Press
Extra! Extra!
Read All About It
Stop the Press
Breaking News
This Just In
The Golden Mail Box Set Books #1-3

The Lucky Billionaire Series
Lucky Break
Streak of Luck
Lucky in Love

The Millionaire's Pretty Woman Series
Perfect Stranger
Captive Devotion
Sweet Temptations

The Sound of Breaking Hearts Series
Disruption
Destroy
Devoted

The University of Gatica Series
The Recruiting Trip
Faster
Higher
Stronger
Dominate
No Rush
University of Gatica - The Complete Series

Timing is Everything Series
Right Time
Right Place
Right Reasons

T.N.T. Series
Troubled Nate Thomas - Part 1
Troubled Nate Thomas - Part 2
Troubled Nate Thomas - Part 3

Toxic Touch Series
Noxious
Lethal
Willful
Tainted
Craved
Toxic Touch Box Set Books #1-3

Undercover Boss Series
Marketing
Finance
Legal

Undercover Series
Perfect For Me
Perfect For You
Perfect For Us

Unknown Identity Series
Unknown
Unpublished
Unexposed
Unsure
Unwritten
Unknown Identity Box Set: Books #1-3

Unlucky Series
Unlucky in Love
UnWanted
UnLoved Forever

War Torn Letters Series
My Sweetheart
My Darling
My Beloved

Wet & Wild Series
Stormy Love
Savage Love
Secure Love

Worth It Series
Worth Billions
Worth Every Cent
Worth More Than Money

You & Me - A Bad Boy Romance
Just Me
Touch Me
Kiss Me

Standalone
Wash
Loving Charity
Summer Lovin'
Love & College
Billionaire Heart
First Love
Frisky and Fun Romance Box Collection
Beating Hades' Bikers
Everyone Loves a Bad Boy
Dead of Night

Watch for more at www.lexytimms.com.

About the Author

"Love should be something that lasts forever, not is lost forever." Visit USA TODAY BESTSELLING AUTHOR, LEXY TIMMS https://www.facebook.com/SavingForever *Please feel free to connect with me and share your comments. I love connecting with my readers.* Sign up for news and updates and freebies - I like spoiling my readers! http://eepurl.com/9i0vD website: www.lexytimms.com Dealing in Antique Jewelry and hanging out with her awesome hubby and three kids, Lexy Timms loves writing in her free time. MANAGING THE BOSSES is a bestselling 10-part series dipping into the lives of Alex Reid and Jamie Connors. Can a secretary really fall for her billionaire boss?

Read more at www.lexytimms.com.

www.ingramcontent.com/pod-product-compliance
Lightning Source LLC
Chambersburg PA
CBHW061517120726
48001CB00004B/1348